PARISIAN SHADOWS

PARISIAN SHADOWS

To: Victoria
Heartfelt thanks for your
support & guidance in
teaching, writing & life
Brian Feb 2025

BRIAN JARMAN

T

Troubador Publishing Ltd
Unit E2 Airfield Business Park,
Harrison Road, Market Harborough,
Leicestershire. LE16 7UL
Tel: 0116 2792299
Email: books@troubador.co.uk
Web: www.troubador.co.uk

ISBN 978 1836282 310

British Library Cataloguing in Publication Data.
A catalogue record for this book is available from the British Library.

Printed and bound in Great Britain by 4edge Limited
Typeset in 11pt Minion Pro by Troubador Publishing Ltd, Leicester, UK

This is dedicated to the cherished memory of Carmen Callil. Her book, *Bad Faith* (2006 Jonathan Cape), inspired this.

1

If this were a film, it would begin with a close-up of the Eiffel Tower lit up on a winter's night. The camera would pan out all the way across the city to the north, to the top of the Parc de Belleville, and then swivel slowly to focus on a small restaurant, Le Vieux Belleville. It's painted cream with a red and white striped awning. It invites you in. From inside comes the sound of a barrel organ and people singing along. It's a simple but haunting refrain, *Trois Petites Notes de Musique*, about the memories a melody can rekindle:

> *Trois petites notes de musique*
> *ont plié boutique au creux du souvenir*
> *C'en est fini de leur tapage*
> *elles tournent la page et vont s'endormir*
> *Mais un jour sans crier gare,*
> *elles vous reviennent en mémoire.*

The camera would pass seamlessly into the interior to reveal a man with an improbably large handlebar moustache, turning the handle of his old wooden barrel organ. Perforated cardboard sheets are folding in front as they pass through the musical mechanism. Diners, sitting at tables covered with red gingham cloths, are joining in with song sheets.

If it were indeed a film, the decor would seem a synthetic set, too much of a cliché of an old Parisian café. The woodwork behind the bar to the left of the door is painted an evocative cream. Among the cupboards with chrome handles like old-fashioned fridges there's a long pull-down baguette drawer. The bar itself is covered with the traditional zinc, on which a handful of older men lean, drinking their aperitifs.

But this is not a film, it's real, old, authentic. The walls are crammed with portraits of singers such as Piaf, Chevalier and Mistinguett, and paintings of the neighbourhood in bygone days. The gingham cloths are covered with labelless bottles of wine, carafes of water, baskets of bread, and plates of rustic food. The organ player changes from the rather melancholic *Trois Petites Notes* to the more upbeat *Quand On S'promène Au Bord de L'eau*, one of those working class Parisian chansons which celebrate Sunday trips to the river at Nogent to the south east of the city.

In the corner by the window opposite the bar, two men sit across from each other, deep in conversation. They've pushed their cheese plates away towards the centre of the table, and are finishing the last of the red wine. They get up, take their overcoats from the stand, and jerk them on. Outside, they shake hands warmly, the one laying his free hand over the wrist of the other. They don't seem to want to leave it at that, and lean in for a rather awkward hug.

The camera follows the slightly shorter one as he approaches the long, narrow flight of stone steps which lead down the side of the park to the little street below. It's a rather misty night now, and a solitary lamp at the bottom casts a rather eerie glow up towards him. He starts his descent with as much confidence as he can muster. In a film, this would signal something bad about to happen. Indeed, it reminds him vaguely of a scene from The Exorcist, he thinks. But he makes it all the way down unscathed and walks briskly down the street through some rather rough-looking blocks of flats. When he reaches the crossroads by the Menilmontant metro station, he breathes more easily: he's on home turf. But then he's hit by a kid on one of those electric scooters that are becoming all the rage. He's not badly hurt, and shouts suitable profanities, but the kid ignores him and whizzes on. Ridiculous things, he thinks. Why can't people walk? They'll eventually lose the use of their legs, and evolve so that they have feet sticking out at the end of their torsos, and waddle along like penguins. He's aware that he's becoming something of a curmudgeon, but he's decided to embrace it rather than fight it. It's probably a losing battle anyway.

He makes his way down rue Oberkampf, still throbbing at this time of night with its many bars and restaurants, until he comes to the front of his apartment building – a typical affair with large wooden double doors. He punches in the code, walks past the bank of letter boxes and into the neat courtyard full of plants in pots. He takes a deep breath better to tackle the three flights of curling stairs to his door. Once inside, he slumps down into the leather club chair and surveys all before him with a sense of satisfaction. It's a mix of IKEA and some art deco pieces he picked up in the market down on boulevard Richard Lenoir which, in his younger days, he lugged up the hill and the stairs. He thinks he should ring Esther and fill her in on the evening's proceedings, but he's too tired. It can wait until the morning. For the moment he wants to bask in the warm feeling of being back in his flat, the flat bequeathed to him by the mysterious aunt he never met. And it's then that the bangs and sirens begin.

2

His upbringing in Aberystwyth was not what you could call run of the mill. His name, for one thing: Steffan Xavier Lewis. Steffan was OK – it would work in Welsh for his father's family, in France for his mother's, and even in English, sort of. But Xavier? There isn't even an X in Welsh, for Christ's sake, and it was a puzzle for the English too. As he grew older he came to dread being asked for his full name, especially in school, but anywhere in Wales when it came down to it.

The use of languages was clearly demarcated, despite his father's worries that it would leave him confused. Young children hoover up different ones without any trouble and know which to use, when and to whom. So it was Welsh in school, English with his father, and French when he was alone with his mother. Of course there was the odd transgression. It became a family joke when he asked his uncle 'Why are you mowing your face like that?' He was sitting on the linen basket in the bathroom, kicking his heels against it and enjoying the novelty of foam and razor – his father used an electric one. In Welsh it's the same word for mow and shave: *torri*. His mother took to saying 'Don't pwn on the table like that,' when he was banging on it, presumably thinking that it was some local English word for thump and not from the Welsh *pwnio*.

His home was a rambling, ramshackle townhouse up near the castle which his parents bought when it was going for a song in the 1950s. They did piecemeal renovations as and when they could afford it, but more often than not these were left unfinished. So the kitchen, for example, remained unfitted: bare boards, plaster of different shades on the walls, a black range that looked positively Victorian but which suited his mother's cuisine, and a cabinet with frosted glass windows at the top and a pull-down shelf for slicing and buttering bread.

As he was growing up in the 1960s, his friends' families had compact modern kitchens in their council houses in Penparcau, velour three-piece suites and swirly carpets. It was a time when plastic was good, wood was bad. He envied these homes, as they were like the ones in the adverts and so something to aspire to. Fish fingers and chips made a welcome change from his mother's robust French cooking. The odd thing was, his best friends Griff and Scooby (so named because of his impressions of the cartoon dog) seemed to enjoy coming to his place too.

'I like your house,' said Scooby one Saturday afternoon, looking around the kitchen.

'Why?' asked Steff. He was just coming up to the age when youngsters express their individuality by trying to be carbon copies of their peers, by conforming.

'Well, it's sort of…different. It's got its own, like, personality.'

That was an important lesson for Steff: you can want to be like someone else while they want to be like you.

They could go and play in the attic where they had a model electric railway, and they didn't baulk at his mother's culinary offerings, although Steff detected discreet sniggers when a whole boiled ox tongue was plonked on the wooden kitchen table, or chicken gizzards served in a salad.

His mother would sometimes slip unwittingly into French with them too.

'Servez-vous!' she would urge, placing a frying pan of some lentil and bacon concoction on a trivet before them, flinging her arms forward in Gallic encouragement.

Indeed it was in large part due to the yeoman loyalty of Griff and Scooby that saved him from oddball isolation in school. He was an only child: they were a lively, likeable trio who were gregarious but also self-contained – rather a winning combination.

Initially it was Griff who was keen on model railways. He'd been given a set for Christmas a few years ago and had been adding to it since, until there was no room for it in his house. On a rainy Saturday afternoon the boys were sitting in the large attic of Steff's house hatching plans, and this conundrum came up. While Scooby and Steff were scratching their heads, Griff suddenly bounded up and said, 'I know. We could have it here. We could just move all this junk to the sides and put it in the middle.' He looked as if it were the best idea in the world, and Scooby joined him in looking expectantly at Steff. He too was intrigued by the idea but his enthusiasm was tempered by a note of caution.

'I'd have to ask Dad,' he said, and his friends demanded that they go downstairs to find him and ask him there and then. 'Yeah, sure,' said his father, and this decision set Steff off indirectly on the path to solve the biggest mystery of his life.

This informal railway club got off to a modest start but soon seemed to take on a life of its own. It began as a bog standard lozenge-shaped layout on the floor, then grew to double, triple its size and acquired loops, branch lines and sidings.

'I know,' said Scooby as they were kneeling on the floor figuring out how they could more easily reach the middle without a delicate hop-scotch over the lines. 'Let's build a kind of table and put it on that. Then we can build mountains and tunnels and bridges and things.'

'How would that work?' asked Steff. 'It'd make it even harder to get to the middle.'

The three sat back on their heels to think.

'We could have a hole in the middle,' said Griff, raising his hand to signal a brainwave. 'Like a sort of donut. Then we could crawl underneath and…and…' He paused to picture what might clinch his argument. 'Have the controls in the centre.'

It was greeted with a few moments of silence.

'How would we do that?' asked Steff, still unsure of the scope of the ambition. None of them particularly shone in woodwork classes.

'We could get your Dad to help.'

His father was known for his DIY around the home, making things himself rather than buying. Sometimes it was rather rough and ready, but had a distinctive style: chunky, wooden, solid.

Steff was still unsure. Yes, his dad was handy but was busy with his teaching job and at home focused on his own projects, which were often months in the making. To Steff's mild surprise he seemed to like the idea when it was put to him that evening.

'Alright,' said his father, 'but you'd have to do all the prep. I can help you design it and do the measurements for the wood and that, but you three would have to get all the materials. OK?'

The boys agreed readily. His friends found in his father something that was missing at home. Griff's never seemed to be there (because he was in the pub, according to his son) and Scooby's was strict and no fun. Steff was a little afraid of him. His own father took his friends under his wing, without making too much of it. When they shyly persisted in calling him Mr Lewis, he said, 'Call me Will.'

And so the grand project began. The boys kept to their end of the bargain and saved up their pocket money to buy the supplies. His father took them to a timber yard and bought wood and lengths of two-by-one for the legs and struts. He was going to get chipboard for the base but Griff said he'd read somewhere that fibreboard was better because it would be easier to pin the track down.

'Fibreboard it is then,' said Will, impressed. They were taking it seriously. Griff beamed with pride. Dismantling the rail network and clearing the attic floor was a long and somewhat dispiriting task, but as the structure took shape so their dreams become a reality. The three boys set to building the base, but Will ended up doing most of the work.

Griff in particular was somewhat daunted by the job.

'I'm not very good at woodwork,' he said, and told Will some story of a collapsed bird box he was responsible for at school.

'Don't worry,' said Will. 'Even the smallest cog helps turn the machine.'

He was given the job of handing him tools, screws, nails and glue and did it with the precision and pride of a scrub nurse. Once the base was finished, the gang stood back and admired it. Then they said they wanted to take it from there. Steff's father took it in good grace and left them to it.

They painted the surface green, re-assembled the network, and then their imagination took flight. They made mountains out of chicken wire, with tunnels and bridges where one loop of the track crossed over another, learning as they went along. They went and gathered little twigs and moss from the hill near the castle to make trees, but soon found that the moss would turn brown. They tried dipping the moss in glue which turned the trees into a gloopy mess, and then varnish, which was just as bad. His mother gave them some of that green stuff for sticking flowers in and that looked better, but still not quite right.

His friends – Grooby as he sometimes thought of them – found a railway magazine in the nearby bookshop and saw an ad for a model shop in Shrewsbury, where you could buy not just trees but people and buildings. They proposed an outing.

Steff had never been on a real train before but because he was now trying to cultivate an air of cool tried to hide rather unsuccessfully his mounting excitement.

They boarded one of the last steam trains to run on the Mid-Wales lines and at first Steff was alarmed at the slight rocking motion and clanking, thinking something was wrong. His friends reassured him that this was perfectly normal.

Once past Constitution Hill the coastal plain from Borth was a little boring but as they climbed up towards Talerddig and crossed the high arch over the road below, their faces were glued to the grimy windows and they caught glimpses of the huge drop through the clouds of steam.

They had the address of the model shop in Milk Street. Griff knew the town slightly as he'd been there shopping with his Mam, but they had to stop two or three times to ask the way as they climbed up the hill and then back down again the other side. When they started the descent, they spotted a Wimpy Bar and egged each other on to go in and have that most exotic of meals, a hamburger, as they'd seen in the movies. Steff had never felt so grown-up.

The shop was exactly as he'd imagined it, without realising he'd imagined anything at all: narrow aisles of floor to ceiling wooden shelves crowded not only with locomotives, carriages, track and signal boxes but also stations and whole villages with green floral foam and stalks for making trees. There was a section of books, and Scooby spent some time thumbing through guides to train spotting. The enthusiasts took their selection of trains, tracks, stations and houses to the large man with a grey beard and half-moon specs behind the tiny counter.

On the way back Scooby sat glued to the train spotting books and did his best to whip up enthusiasm in the others to adopt the hobby and come back to Shrewsbury to start underlining the train numbers in the lists. Steff was silently sceptical that it was his thing. The next day they set to, laying the extra track, constructing a new station and a village surrounding it, and building more mountains out of chicken wire and papier maché. It became clear that they would need to extend the base to accommodate all of the track.

Scooby though was raring to start spotting trains and so the three set off a couple of weeks later with sandwiches and thermoses and spent the day on Shrewsbury station in their anoraks against the drizzle and pencilled under the numbers of locomotives passing through. Scooby seemed in his element, Griff showed willing, but to Steff it was misery.

He excused himself from the trip to Birmingham New Street the next Saturday, saying truthfully he wanted to continue the development of the railway. This entailed adding a new section to the wooden base and it was to this end that he set about dragging a rusty tin trunk from the end wall to the far corner of the opposite one. As he did so, an old book that was behind it flopped to the ground.

He paused to pick it up. It was a photo album. There were others in the sideboard drawer downstairs charting his childhood with his parents and friends on beaches, on hilltops, on his grandparents' farm. This one was clearly much older, full of little square monochrome snapshots slotted into cut-out corners on black pages. Some of the corners were broken and a few photos tumbled out onto his knees. He picked them up and crouched down to take a closer look. The fashions were of the 1920s with women wearing dresses down to their shins and cloche hats. In several of them he recognised his grandparents in Paris, standing in a group by a river – there were a couple of such photos in the albums downstairs. They were with his mother when she must have been about four or five, and also another girl probably a couple of years older. He pondered for a minute or so. She must be the mysterious aunt he had never met, Céleste, of whom he had only ever heard spoken about in whispers.

3

He recognised the house the instant he saw it: it was just like Meulisnart, Captain Haddock's house in the Tintin books (or whatever it was in English – he'd read them in both languages and even one in Welsh). He'd loved them when he was younger and, truth be known, he sometimes still read them secretly in his bed at night when he needed comfort. Whether the memory, fixed in his mind's eye like a photo he now realised, came from a previous visit or from the old album, he couldn't tell.

His mother had told him that she and his father had taken him to see his French grandparents when he was a babe in arms. And then there'd been another visit when he was six or seven with just his mother. Some of the memories of this time were sharp and clear, if brief, while others were misty. What he did remember vaguely were hushed conversations when he was out of the room but listening at the door. Many of the sentences began with 'Elle…' but, strain as he might, he couldn't catch anything that shed more light on the mystery that he now understood to be his Tata Céleste. Fragments: 'pas de contacte,' 'jamais,' 'on sait pas.'

This time he was curious to know more about her but didn't know how he could go about it. When he'd shown his mother that photo he found in the attic and asked her who it was, her reply was curt: 'My sister.' When he asked for more information about her, she said 'We haven't talked for years,' and her tone suggested that was all she was going to say on the matter. She wouldn't tell him why. He learned that it was not a good idea to ask questions about this aunt he'd never known about.

A year or two after this his mother had brought up the idea of visiting her parents just outside Paris in the school holidays: her parents were not getting any younger and who knew when...

Steff got the impression that whether his father would accompany them became a bone of contention between his parents. Even though they didn't discuss it in front of him, he somehow gleaned, as children can, that his father didn't want to go, and his mother wanted him to. When he and his father went for a walk along the beach, Steff asked him why he wasn't coming with them. His father looked uncomfortable and mumbled something about being too busy, although Steff couldn't see at what.

He himself was keen on the trip. The train trio had finished the model railway to their great joy, but the Grooby were spending more time gallivanting to stations around the country collecting engine numbers in their little books. Steff had no stomach for it, and at times felt their enthusiasm for rail was beginning to outgrow his. He would welcome a break. And maybe he'd find out more about the puzzling aunt.

It would be a long journey. His father suggested they spend a couple of days in London so Steff could see the sights. They could stay with a distant relative of his who ran a boarding house in Paddington, Aunty Polly.

'Very well,' said his mother, but did so without much enthusiasm. His father left the kitchen singing *Pretty Little Polly Perkins from Paddington Green*.

He was surprised at how well his mother seemed to know London, as they hopped on a bus at Euston which would take them to Paddington. His aunt's place was called Wycombe House, which for Steff had taken on a whole atmosphere of its own over the years as he heard his parents mention it, an atmosphere he could almost taste, even though he had never been there. The mere mention of those two words evoked for him the glamour and sophistication of London.

'You forget I lived here for two years during the war,' she said, and from the top of the bus pointed out the hostel where she stayed. 'That's when I met your father and then he whisked me off to Wales.'

Steff thought this might be a good time to ask about her sister but by the time he'd plucked up the courage they'd reached their stop.

Aunty Polly was a lean, severe and taciturn woman who, after a cursory enquiry after his father, showed them to their rooms. It was a far cry from the picture Steff had formed in his mind – an old and shabby house whose dominant tone was brown and cream paint. His aunt clearly did not hold with small talk, much to Steff's relief and, he thought, to that of his mother. He suspected she'd come across Aunty P before as he sensed some mutual antagonism between them.

She spent the next day and a half showing him the famed landmarks. He liked the Houses of Parliament best. They mostly walked, but took a couple of tube rides for the experience. He immediately took to the busyness and bustle of the place, felt its magic.

'Which do you like best, London or Paris?' he asked her as they strolled down the Mall. His mother had a ready-made answer.

'London for its character, Paris for its beauty,' she said, puffing contentedly on her Disque Bleu which she'd found in an old tobacconist's. It was a smell he forever associated with her. He knew what she meant about London's character. He had yet to appreciate the beauty of Paris.

'It's not exactly Versailles,' she said, when they reached Buckingham Palace for the Changing of the Guard. 'But I like it better. *Le style Britannique.*'

Then it was a short walk down to Victoria for the boat train and the night ferry to Calais. As they settled down into their seats and made themselves as comfortable as they could for the crossing, Steff told himself it was now or never if he was to find out more about Céleste. He'd need to know what to say or more likely not to say around his grandparents.

After his mother had reacted so oddly to the photo, he hadn't mentioned it to her again. He'd put it back in the album and stuffed it behind the trunk. He'd briefly wondered it he should ask his father, but something held him back.

'So what happened to you and Tante Céleste?' he said. 'I'm guessing I shouldn't mention her around the grandparents.' He saw his mother bridle a little, and he immediately regretted that '*tante*.' He couldn't have said what made him do it. But his mother seemed to take a deep breath.

'Alright, I'll tell you what I know, but that's not much. She cut herself off from the family years ago.'

The sisters were close growing up in that rambling house on the banks of the Seine at Conflans, said his mother. They were still on good terms when his mother left for London in 1938 to do a teacher training course. Her sister, three years older, was already teaching at a lycée in Paris near the Père Lachaise cemetery. She had a small studio apartment nearby but spent the weekends with her parents in Conflans-Sainte-Honorine, where the Seine joined the Oise west of the capital. Then came the war when it was difficult to keep in touch. Céleste stopped coming to Conflans at weekends. When Paris was liberated and she would have been able go to see her parents again, they'd lost touch with her. She must have moved out of the flat she had in Paris: when they went to find her it was occupied by someone else and there was no forwarding address.

'What about her school? Did they try that?'

'Of course,' said Camille. 'But same thing – she'd moved on and they didn't know where. You must remember that things were pretty chaotic in Paris after the war. People were displaced, went missing, records were lost.'

'Did Papie and Mamie even know she was alive?'

'They had one postcard about six months after the liberation. It said something like 'I'm alive and well. Don't worry about me.' She took a drag on her cigarette. 'That was it.'

There was anger and bitterness in her voice.

'Did you always get on with her before that?'

There was something a little furtive in the look on her face, thought Steff.

'We were just normal sisters, you know. Played together, fought together. She was considered the sensible one, a little reserved. I was the wild one, so as we grew up we started going our separate ways. But, yes, we never had a big falling out. Now, chéri, I'm tired. Let's try to get some sleep.'

It was frustrating. Maybe he'd get some more information from his grandparents. Surely someone, somewhere, must know something.

His grandmother greeted him with kisses on both cheeks (as did his whiskery grandfather) and the customary words that teenagers find boring or embarrassing: 'How you've grown! You were just this high when I last saw you.' 'What are you doing at school?' 'Have you got a girlfriend yet?' She called him Stéphane, which he didn't like. She was tiny and wore a mustard cardigan over some kind of flowery housecoat. Her hair was a white bob, tinged with orange at the ends. His mother told him she dyed it with coffee. She had a precise way of talking, annunciating each word slowly and clearly. At first he thought she'd forgotten he was fluent in French but then noticed this was how she spoke to everyone. In fact everything she did was precise, measured, serious. She was thin as if she wasn't eating properly. She seemed nervy.

'And Camille,' she said and there was another round of kisses. 'How lovely to see you. You don't come to see us often enough.' The half-smile on her pinched lips seemed forced.

'Well, we're here now so let's enjoy it.'

His grandfather didn't have much to say for himself. He was, thought Steff, typically French: short with a droopy white moustache, tinged with yellow as it reached his mouth from where a strong untipped cigarette usually dangled. He was something of a shadowy figure and, once the customary salutations were over, disappeared to the garage, or garden, or some inner sanctum.

The house was as he vaguely remembered it: full of solid wooden furniture, quite dark as there was heavy lace on the windows, a bit fussy as he thought of it. There was oilcloth covered with lace on the large round kitchen table where they ate on the dot of the proper time, and where his Mamie seemed to spend almost the entire day. Unlike the kitchen at home, everything had its place and that's where it had to be. But there were things missing: they had no kettle (probably because they didn't drink tea and had an old fashioned enamel cafetière for their coffee) and no toaster, although he imagined it would have been odd to have one in the shape of the baguettes Mamie went out to buy each morning. In fact her day seemed one endless round of chores with which his grandfather seemed to do nothing to help: shopping, cooking, cleaning, washing, making the fires.

It had been quite a grand house in its time, but was way past its prime. He contrasted it with that of his Welsh grandparents, on a remote hill farm: two up, two down, no bathroom, no electricity, no running water. Instead there was a tin bath hanging on the outside wall, oil lamps, and a hand pump in the yard at which Steff had spent hours when young to fill up buckets. It was the happiest of times, the happiest of places. He adored his grandmother in particular. She always greeted him with the words, '*Ac o ble daethwyt ti, te*? (And where did you spring from?), which became music to his ears.

He was given a bedroom at the back corner of the house with sweeping views down to the river and the plains the other side. It was a monk's cell of a room, a single bed with an iron bedstead and a dreary old wallpaper. No accessories of any kind. His mother had the counterpart at the opposite corner, beyond the bathroom with brass taps and dark green brick-shaped tiles half way up the wall. Her room had more in it – bookshelves on the wall, a couple of ancient prints of the town, a desk with a lamp. He took it that it was her old room, and he was in Céleste's, but by this time he knew far better than to ask.

He noticed his mother behaved differently in her parents' house to the lively, spirited person he knew. She seemed subservient to them, fitting in with their fixed routines but seemed resentful that she had to do so and was often mildly impatient with them. There was something in the house that made Steff uneasy, like a bad smell that catches the back of your nose at odd moments, but was gone before you could identify it.

He bided his time to broach the subject of his aunt. It came a couple of days after their arrival, at the four o'clock snack Mamie called *gouter* – coffee and *langue de chat* biscuits. Much to her annoyance, his grandfather was in the garden and didn't come when he was called, and his mother had gone for a walk into the centre of Conflans. He'd declined her invitation to join her in order to be alone with this grandmother.

'I found an old photo in the attic a while back of Maman and her sister.'

He waited for Mamie to respond but she didn't. She seemed to be concentrating on sipping her coffee in a ladylike manner. She had the same look as that of his mother when he'd mentioned his aunt on the ferry.

'Maman said she hasn't been in touch with anyone since before the war.'

'No,' she said through pursed lips, placing her little cup carefully on its saucer. This wasn't going to be easy.

'Do you know why, Mamie?'

'How could I? There's been no communication.'

'But you don't have an inkling (he used the word *soupçon*)? Or didn't then?'

She took a deep breath and seemed to accept that she owed him some explanation, as meagre as it was.

'No, she was here one weekend as normal. No sign of anything wrong. She looked a bit wrung out, of course, but it was the war. Then nothing. Ever again. Well, one postcard after the war was over.'

'Did she know about me?'

'How on earth could she? This was years before you were born.'

She shifted her position on her chair and straightened her back, as if to signal the end of the matter. She looked at him.

'There's a young couple next door now. He's French, from near here, but she's English too.'

Steff didn't like that 'too.' He knew the French would often say English when they meant British, but he only ever thought of himself as Welsh.

'*Moi, j'suis gallois, pas anglais,*' he said

Mamie simply smiled weakly and nodded, as if to say yes, yes, whatever.

The house next door was modern with a flat roof: a white box. Steff liked it, partly because of the stark contrast to the Tintin house, but they both had steep gardens sweeping down to the river. He took to hanging around in the garden when he could in the hope of meeting the English too woman. He had a vague notion that she might know something about Céleste, albeit he couldn't have said exactly how that would have happened. He sat on the terrace in front of the house, where there was an outdoor dining table under vine leaves. Why didn't they eat there, he wondered? It was certainly hot enough. Yet he knew why: his grandparents had their ways and were set in them. They didn't appear to like the sun, although his Papie loved pottering in the garden. He kept one eye on the windows of the white box but saw no movement. He learnt later from his Mamie that they were both teachers so were out all day.

His mother wanted to show him Paris so for a couple of days running they took the train into Saint Lazare and did a tour of the sights as they had in London. He could appreciate the beauty of Paris that his mother had spoken of, but above all he loved the cafés and the mouthwatering shops – the *boulangeries*, the *fruits et légumes* with their artistically stacked products, the prepared food of the *traiteurs* which had no counterpart at home. They sat on café terraces and indulged in the time-honoured pastime of watching Paris go by. She sipped a kir, he was allowed a *demi*. Even though he spoke French to his mother most of the time, it was odd to hear everyone around him doing the same – quite a difference between the intimate chats between just the two of them and the everyday chatter of the streets. And then there were the latest phrases that neither of them were up on, such as '*chansons yéyé*,' meaning the contemporary pop music. They discussed this when they heard it and surmised it came from yeah yeah.

'Some of it is quite pleasant,' said his mother. 'But I prefer my Piaf.'

She told him how in recent years she'd tried to update her style to appeal to a younger audience, but it didn't quite work.

'The old ones are the best,' she said. 'Speaking of which, let's go and see her grave. Hers was one of the biggest funerals Paris has ever seen. It's just up the road.'

Steff was startled.

'We're in Paris and you're taking me to see *dead people?*'

'You'll see,' she said with a knowing smile, and marched him up the avenue de la République towards the Père Lachaise cemetery.

He did see. It turned out to be one of the highlights of the visits. He found the place fascinating, with its undulating avenues twisting through trees, the little houses covering the older, richer family vaults, the photos of the dear departed on the tombstones. It had a special atmosphere of peace. Some young people were even having a picnic on one of the old graves, swigging from a bottle of red wine. An old guy had sold them a map of the plots of the famous at the gate for a few centimes. They made straight for Piaf's grave. It looked a fairly simple affair, although it was still heaped with flowers a couple of years after her burial, a photo of her on the headstone, a common practice in French graveyards, which he found odd. Little details can make a huge difference.

They followed the map and found the graves of Chopin, Wilde, Bernhardt and many more. His mother took him to the Communards' Wall – where some hundred and fifty of them had been lined up and shot. They were part of the short-lived revolution after the Franco-Prussian war of 1870 whereby the people declared Paris a war-free zone. From there they went on to the holocaust memorials to the Jews deported from Paris to the death camps in the Second World War. Steff was particularly struck by the Buchenwald statue, three screaming skeletal people piled on top of each other. His mother stood in silence for quite a time, eventually turning away, brushing her eye and saying, 'To think all that happened here.'

As they were walking back down the avenue de la République, his mother nodded towards a large austere old building on the other side of the street and remarked casually: 'That's where your aunt taught.'

Steff stopped in his tracks.

'What?' He stared at the lycée. It tingled his spine to think that this real, solid, present-day school once employed the mysterious woman that was his aunt.

'Let's go in and see if we can find out anything about her,' he said.

'There's no point,' said his mother, wearily blowing out her cigarette smoke.

'Why not?'

'Your grandparents did all that after the war. They went to the school and trudged around the area trying to find any tiny clue as to her whereabouts. The school said they had no records. They must have been destroyed in the war or something.'

Steff was reluctant to leave the spot.

'Come on, chéri. It's all in the past. It's over now.'

He was beginning to think that there was something someone was not telling him.

It was a couple of days after this that he managed to speak to the English too woman next door. She was laying their terrace table for dinner, just as he wanted to happen his side of the fence. He kicked his heels for a while, hoping she'd notice him. When she didn't, he called out to her.

'Hello there,' he said in English, giving her a wave.

'Ooh hello,' she said, and he decided on the spot that she was a nice, friendly person. They introduced themselves and he found that she was Rita, originally from Manchester, and a teacher in a local *collège*. She seemed to take to him too.

'Come round for an *apéro*,' she said. 'In about an hour. Bob will be home by then.' She must have seen Steff look blank. 'He's my husband.'

'I thought he was French?'

'Oh, he is. His name's Robert. I just call him Bob.'

Steff knew that an aperitif was a drink you had before a meal, but he'd never had one, let alone been invited for one. Maybe Rita thought he was older than he was. Or maybe she didn't care. In any event, he was determined to go. Dinner at his grandparents' was at eight sharp – two hours away so there would be plenty of time. He fairly bounced back up to the kitchen where he announced his invitation to his family.

Mamie looked put out, and his mother asked what time *they* would be going.

'It was only me that was asked, Mum. Don't embarrass me.'

His mother shrugged, bowing to the inevitable.

'Alright then, but just one drink.'

'What do you have for an aperitif then?'

'Spirits usually. See if they've got pastis. That's like an aniseed liqueur but make sure there's plenty of water in it.'

Steff had never felt so sophisticated as when he approached the front door of the white house later that evening, armed with a long thin saucisson that Mamie had insisted he took because it was not the done thing for a guest to arrive empty-handed. Rita greeted him like an old friend.

'Come in, come in,' she said, sweeping her arm inwards. 'Or rather, come out. We're in the garden.'

He followed her through the lounge which was also painted white, lined floor to ceiling with bookshelves and paintings of all descriptions. Jazz was playing somewhere in the background. They went down a winding staircase to their terrace below, where Bob, he assumed, was drinking a whisky. He got up, shook Steff's hand, and motioned to one of the iron seats around the table.

'What would you like to drink?' he said in English.

'A pastis please,' said Steff, grateful for his mother's advice.

'I'll have one too,' said Rita.

Bob took two tall glasses from the tray of drinks on the table and poured a little Ricard in each. He picked up a jug of water.

'Say when.'

Steff let him fill his glass almost to the top.

'*Des glaçons?*'

'*Oui, je veux bien.*'

'There's not much room,' said Bob with a smirk. 'Is that for us?' nodding at the saucisson which Steff was still nursing.

'Oh yes,' said Steff handing it over.

Rita set about slicing it into thin *rondelles* and added them to a wooden platter laden with pistachios and little cubes of flavoured cheese wrapped in foil. She went to find some little gherkins to go with the meat. The three talked easily as they found out about each other. Steff felt relaxed with them: they were natural and funny and treated him as an equal without asking about school and girlfriends and offered him Gauloises which he declined. They stuck mainly to English with the odd phrase in French. Bob was fluent, with a discernible northern accent (he'd taught in a school in Leeds for a number of years which was where he met Rita) with some slight French intonation now and then. Steff finished his pastis – he'd loved aniseed balls as a youngster – and Bob without asking gave him a refill, pouring in more this time.

Steff had been trying to figure out how to bring up the subject of his missing aunt but the couple were so easy-going that he saw no reason to beat around the bush.

'How long have you lived here?'

'About ten years now,' said Bob.

'Do you know my grandparents?'

The two glanced briefly at each other.

'Not well,' said Rita. 'We know them to say hello to when we're in the garden but they kind of keep themselves to themselves. They don't seem to go out much.'

'Did you know that they have another daughter, Céleste?'

'I think we did know that,' said Rita. 'I don't know how. But we've never met her.' She was looking at him somewhat quizzically. Bob said something about another neighbour mentioning the fact to them at some point, but was rather vague about who or when. Steff could not think how to pursue the matter, but once again was left unsatisfied that he'd found out all that there was to know.

'Well, we're going to eat now,' said Rita eventually.

'It's choucroute garnie – why don't you join us?'

Steff would have loved to. Apart from anything else it was one of his favourite dishes which his mother made: sauerkraut with sausages and ham hock. But he felt honour bound to say he was expected next door. He glanced at his watch and saw to his dismay that he was already thirty minutes late. He stood up to go.

'How long are you here for?' asked Rita.

'About another week, I think.'

'Well, come and see us again. See if you can get a pass to come and eat with us.'

Steff promised he would and made his way a little tipsily back, bracing himself for the censure that was awaiting him.

4

It was shortly after their return to Wales that Steff, in the eyes of his parents and teachers at least, started to go off the rails, so to speak. The Grooby still came around once in a while to operate the attic railway. They'd gone at it full throttle, forming a model railway club at school and spending many weeks travelling the country to spot trains. Steff began to develop interests elsewhere. His old friends would still come round sometimes on rainy Saturdays when it was just too miserable to stand on railway platforms. Steff was quite willing to go along with them and keep the railway in good running order and carry out maintenance. But they were perplexed and miffed that he didn't want to join in with all their activities.

'Why don't you want to come to the school club,' asked Griff on one such afternoon. 'The set is getting quite big now. We could do with your help.'

'I dunno,' said Steff. 'Got other fish to fry.'

The truth of it was, he'd got a new friend: Johnny Fitzakerley, known as Fitz. He came from Liverpool and his mother ran a pub in the town, The Cambrian Arms.

Fitz had all the wit and street wisdom of his native city and Steff took to him immediately as a big brother. He failed to see though why Fitz bothered with him. Steff had always been at or near the top of his class, but Fitz for all his worldliness was no scholar. About this time Steff was getting a little bored by some of his O level subjects, particularly French. The school had no option for fluent speakers, as they did in Welsh, so he had to take the standard course. He enjoyed aspects such as translation from one language to the other as there was an art to getting it just right, but the learning of vocabulary and grammar was just tedious for him as it was redundant. For this reason his teacher, nicknamed Powder Puff because of her heavy make-up, had taken a dislike to him and the feeling was mutual. She passed herself off as French but Steff knew she wasn't.

'In France they hate broad beans,' she told the class for some reason one morning. 'We throw them to the pigs.'

Steff couldn't resist.

'Please miss, do you eat broad beans?'

'Oh, I have a Welsh husband who loves them,' she said with a trill of a laugh but gave him an odd look.

Steff had found out she came from Swansea.

As she was giving back the homework she'd marked she ticked them off soundly, in her odd accent with its vague twang which was somewhere between French and American.

'It's about time you pulled your socks up,' she bellowed. She was rather formidable. So of course Steff bent forward in his seat and performed the action. Powder

Puff banished him to the lower class, CSE. Here he sat next to Fitz and was quite happy to do so. He knew he could get a top grade here, which would count as an O level, and the last thing he wanted to do was to go to Powder Puff and beg her to take him back. He and Fitz became as thick and thieves, and he felt he was learning things from him that no book could teach him.

It was near the end of the spring term when things were winding down that Fitz said they should skive off the French class. Steff didn't want to appear a swot so he went along with him. First they stopped off at The Cambrian Arms – it was before opening time – and Fitz showed him how to work the whisky optic. Steff wasn't keen on it but drank it, trying not to screw up his face too much.

'Another?' asked Fitz.

'Isn't it opening time soon?'

'Oh, yeah. Me mam'll be down soon. We'd better scarper.'

He led the way to a ramshackle garage behind the pub where his brother kept his motor bike. Steff thought this was taking things a bit far – they could get in serious trouble – but he could hardly pull out now. He had no choice but to get on the back behind Fitz who turned out to be a very good driver. They took the quiet back streets towards the hill that ran past Bronglais Hospital and then on to a steep field under the woods. There were what appeared to be bike tracks up through the trees so Steff thought it must be a favourite Fitzakerley trail. After a couple of circuits Fitz gave him a go, showing him how to control the throttle and brakes. It was a bit jerky at first but he soon started getting the hang of it.

'Don't get stuck in the ruts,' shouted Fitz. 'Get on to clean ground if they're too deep.'

It was an exhilarating time for Steff, like nothing he'd ever known. He did feel a little guilty but sort of liked that feeling. He realised as well, though, that this could be a slippery path if they were to make a habit of it. But he soon had another distraction. A new girl came to town, who was also from away, from somewhere in England although he could never pin her down to exactly where. He couldn't have said that he was seeking friends from far away with any degree of deliberation but both Fitz and Jill seemed to hold some kind of fascination for him. She was tiny, with light brown hair down to her waist and a cheeky smile. He fell for her at first sight, and they took to meeting up every dinnertime and going to a dark passageway behind some old houses which were boarded up for what they would have termed snogging and suchlike. He lavished her with gifts, but as he was new to this they were probably not the best choice for a teenager. He bought her a brush, hand mirror and comb set in a box which would have been more appropriate for his mother or even grandmother. She looked pleased, though, and he didn't care that she gave him nothing. Then there was a cheap ring from Woolworth's and a pen and pencil set.

He was grateful that the school had not communicated his demotion to his parents, but they must have sensed that he was not taking his studies seriously. Even though they were both educators, or maybe because of it, they didn't push him.

'How's school?' his father asked him when he came down to supper one evening.

'OK.'

'Anything wrong?'

'Nope.'

'It's just that you don't seem to be yourself recently. You're out a lot in the evening and your mother and I are concerned about you. We don't think you're paying enough attention to your schoolwork.'

'There's nothing wrong.'

'Well remember that you can always come to talk to us if there is. Now's the time to apply yourself at school. Your qualifications are the passport to the life you want to lead.'

His words struck a minor chord with Steff. And two things happened shortly afterwards that would change his course again. Jill vanished from the town without a word to him and without a trace. He never knew what happened to her, despite making some desultory enquiries around the town, and never heard of her again. And as exams approached his CSE teacher Miss Evans (who had not been at the school long enough to acquire a nickname) told him at the beginning of class one day that he should go to apologise to Powder Puff and ask if he could come back to the O level class. He slouched into the room and said 'Miss Evans says I should come back to you and say sorry.'

'Sit down,' she said, and went on with the class.

It was the arrival of Caroline, or Caro as she said they could call her, in the Lower Sixth form that helped set him back on track. She was an *assistante,* who took his class for conversation lessons. Of course his French was more or less fluent and far in advance of his classmates', but he tried to hold back and not show off too much. He did learn though, because her French was more up to date than his mother's: Caro would say *une boum* for a party whereas he'd learnt to say *une fête.* They hit it off immediately. She had a mischievous sense of humour. They went on a school trip to Machynlleth to see a production of Henry V, where he defeats the French army at Agincourt. They sat together on the bus and developed a strange system whereby she'd speak to him in English and he'd reply in French. That way they could both practise what they needed to. She wanted him to tell her as much as he could about the culture, language and history of Wales, which she professed to have fallen in love with. He taught her a few phrases in Welsh and her accent was pretty good. She taught him some puns in French: if you say Shakespeare with a French accent it sounds like 'the dying cat' (*chat q'expire*) which could be expressed as *Minetquimeurt* (the perishing pussy).

His mother had the idea that he should go to spend the summer with his grandparents in Conflans which did not fill him with delight. On the spur of the moment he approached Caro one morning after class and asked her how he could find a job in France for the summer. She thought about it for a moment.

'Maybe you could come and stay with my family. I'll ask them.'

It was all arranged after the next class. Her parents lived in Beauvais in Picardy. He could share a room with her brother, Jean Claude, who was a couple of years older. They wouldn't charge much for board and lodging. He jumped at the chance. But he'd have to break it to his mother.

'Maman, you know I've told you about Caro, the *assistante,*' he said that evening as his mother was stirring something in a large pan on the stove.

'I seem to remember you've mentioned her once or twice.' He could tell she was being ironic. He must have been going on about her somewhat.

'Well, she's invited me to stay with her family in Beauvais for the summer.'

She stopped mid stir, turned around and stared at him.

'But what about your grandparents? I've already talked to them. They'll be bitterly disappointed.'

'Aw, come on, Maman. They'll hardly charge me anything and I can find a job.'

'Your grandparents won't charge you anything.'

Steff had been working on his killer argument.

'If I went to Caro's family it would help me with my A levels. She's studying English at university, so we can talk about the set books I have to do. And I can go and visit Mamie and Papie.'

It took his mother a while to come around, but eventually she reluctantly seemed to concede that she couldn't order him to go to her parents.

The next summer he and Caro took the train to London, then down to Gatwick to get a Dan-Air flight to Beauvais. Her parents' flat was in a huge, modern housing development of HLMs – the equivalent of council housing – on a plateau on the northern outskirts of the city. He felt at home straightaway. Her parents, Albert and Monique, were factory workers and Steff could see where Caro got her sense of humour from: her father was a joker. He'd tell Steff slang phrases which sounded odd coming out of the mouth of a well-mannered young foreigner.

'In Picardy we don't say *merci*, we say *merdeci*,' he said one evening when they were having an aperitif in a nearby café (*merde* meaning shit). 'And it's more polite to say *un coup d'rouge,* when you ask for a glass of red wine, not *un verre de vin rouge.'*

Steff wondered why Albert, Jean-Claude, and the waiter laughed when he ordered. It turned out that *un coup d'rouge* was considered rather vulgar, roughly the equivalent to 'a slug of red.' But he took it in good part.

At weekends he'd go out with Jean-Claude and his friends, one of whom had a car. They seemed content to drive around, maybe stop in a café to play *flipper* (pinball) and sip coffee or Orangina, rarely beer. Steff thought of his friends back home who'd probably be sitting in a pub getting drunk. Caro too drove him around to various places. On one such drive, after he'd been there a couple of weeks or so, he brought up the subject of finding work.

'Realistically, I think it'll be hard for you to find a job for a month.'

He knew she had a point, but couldn't help wondering why she hadn't warned him before. He'd imagined working in a café but learned that being a waiter was quite a sought-after occupation in France and it took time to be trained properly. Her parents had both asked at their factories but there was nothing going. Well, so be it. He had enough savings to pay his way out. He suspected that Caro preferred him being around so they could keep up their bilingual chatter and learn from each other.

On one of these outings, Caro took him to see her grandmother, Albert's mother, who lived in a little old house on the way down to the town. She was like a granny from a storybook: tiny with tight, white curls and a squeaky voice. Her head made little jerky bird-like movements as she talked. She welcomed Steff as if he were a long lost member of the family, taking his hand in hers and patting it.

'Ah, the English are so cold,' she warbled. 'Don't you find? Never mind, I'll be your grandmother while you're here.' He felt a little guilty that he found her easier going than his own grandmother. Even at her time of life she seemed to enjoy it, determined to get the most out of it.

It was late afternoon and she served them small glasses of port.

'You English like port, don't you?'

Steff and Caro exchanged glances, and the silent consensus was that it would be pointless to try to explain about the Welsh. Steff, who had never tasted port, said, 'Yes.'

Like her son and granddaughter, she had a keen sense of humour, and her forte was the French equivalent of knock knock jokes.

'*Monsieur et Madame Enfaillite ont une fille. Comment l'appelleront ils?*'

Caro looked wearily out of the window. She must have heard this dozens of times. Steff had to admit he didn't know.

'*Melusine.*'

It took him a moment to work out that this would give the daughter the preposterous name Melusine Enfaillite, translating roughly as Bankrupt the Factory. Was it worth the effort, he wondered, but forced a little laugh. This just encouraged the grandmother to trot out some more, even unfunnier. Her room put him in mind of his grandparents' house: heavy wooden furniture, lace, yellowing patterned wallpaper.

He hadn't forgotten the promise to his mother, and was as good as his word. And he was not insensible to the hope that one of the neighbours might be able to shed some little light on the aunt mystery. He took a train to Paris and then out to Conflans for a few days. He was prepared for a frosty reception but his grandmother seemed her normal self, which was somewhat reserved at the best of times. No mention was made of his decision to spend the summer with strangers, apart from, 'Are you getting on OK where you are?'

Steff thought it wise to confine himself to: 'Yes, all's good.'

He looked around the kitchen.

'Your grandfather's in the garden as usual, I think. You can go to say hello.'

He wandered out and found him hoeing a vegetable patch towards the bottom of the garden where it flattened out as it neared the river. There were brief kisses and words of greeting, then his grandfather went back to his hoeing.

As he trudged up the steps back to the house, he caught sight of Rita stretched out on a lounger reading. He went over to the fence and waved hello.

'Well, hello there,' she said putting down her book. 'A Tale of Two Cities. It's my project for the summer. Getting through as much Dickens as I can. Have you read it?'

'No,' said Steff.

'You should. I'll give it to you when I've finished. It'll make me get a move on.'

She seemed genuinely pleased to see him and came over to her side of the fence.

'Come over for an aperitif.'

'Just got here,' he said. 'Better stay with the old folks tonight.'

'Come for dinner tomorrow night then. I'm sure it would be alright if you gave enough notice. They can't expect you to stay with them every hour God sends, can they?'

Steff was pretty sure they could, or at least his grandmother could. She'd probably been planning every meal since he told them he was coming. But he couldn't pass this up. He'd given some thought about what he'd say to Rita when they met again. About the aunt. Now was the time to be open.

'OK. You know, I've been thinking what you said last time, about one of the neighbours remembering my aunt. Can you think who it would be?'

'No,' said Rita, frowning, 'fraid not. How old would your aunt be now?'

'Let's see. She's a couple of years older than my mother, so about fiftyish.'

'Hmm. We could try Sophie. She's about that age. She grew up down the street and then went to live in Paris. She was a teacher. She moved back after her parents died.'

'My aunt was a teacher in Paris,' said Steff, beginning to feel a thrill of expectation.

'Well that could work. Tell you what, if you come over tomorrow night, I'll see if she and her husband are free and I'll invite them too.'

Mamie remained even tighter-lipped than usual when he told her about his plans, merely giving a lopsided shrug and spreading her hands out as if to say, 'Off you go then. What can I do about it?'

Papie was nowhere to be seen, but emerged at the prescribed hour for dinner and they sat down to pâté and cassoulet, followed (as always) by dressed lettuce and cheese. Conversation was sparse, as all three of them seemed to be running out of things to say. Steff wished he was next door.

The next evening his grandfather took him down to the cellar where he kept his wine so as to pick out a bottle he could take to the neighbours. Steff knew a little about French wines, as they often had some at home, and knew that it was important to pair wine with food.

'Do you know what they're serving?' he asked.

Steff wondered out loud how he could.

'Oh well, let's go for a Gamay. That's pretty versatile. I've got some good ones from the Tours region.'

It was the most animated and talkative he'd seen his grandfather. While he was rummaging around selecting a dusty bottle from the racks, Steff looked around the cellar. It had an old roll-top desk stuffed with papers and neat rows of various tools hanging from hooks. This was probably the inner sanctum, he thought.

He found Rita and Bob sitting at the garden table in the evening sun, already coiffing their whisky and pastis. It was seven o'clock and he wondered if he should have come earlier, but the couple seemed nonchalant about the timings of things, unlike their next door neighbours.

'*Ah, monsieur le gallois,*' said Bob, rising to his feet and shaking his hand. He poured him a stiff pastis and Rita brought out her trademark platter of nibbles.

'Good news,' she said. 'Sophie and her husband Bernard are coming so you can ask them about your missing aunt.'

At that, the doorbell rang and in came Sophie and Bernard. She was an elegant woman, with short neatly-coiffed fair hair. He was tall with a vaguely military bearing. The conversation switched to French.

It was a convivial evening, with scrumptious food. The main dish was *choucroute garnie,* which Steff thought was the best he'd ever had. The wine and banter flowed, and it was clear that the two couples understood each other well and shared a sense of humour. Steff wasn't clear how much Sophie knew about his family, or how to ask, but it was she who brought up the matter first.

'I remember your aunt when we were kids,' she said as they started on the cheese. 'I think she was a year or two younger than me, so we weren't in the same class at school, but we knew each other from playing in the street, which we did back then, before the war. And we went to each other's birthday parties. But 1 couldn't say we were best friends or anything.'

'Did you know my mother too?'

'Of course she'd be that much younger again so I didn't know her so well. You know how kids are – it's beneath them to mix with those in classes two or three years below. I think I can remember her vaguely though. Occasionally she would play with us but had playmates her own age. She was more outgoing, a bit of a live wire. Is she well?'

'Yes, very, thank you. She's a teacher now. And what was my aunt like?'

'To tell the truth, she was a little reserved. Not a pack leader, as it were. Happy to follow.'

Steff sensed there was more to come. Sophie paused as if making up her mind to tell all. She did.

'But as she got older I don't think she was happy.'

'Why not?'

'Well, as I say, she didn't open up much. But I got the impression things weren't good at home. Her parents were quite strict, rigid. Especially her father. The word she used for him was *sévere*.'

'Did you keep in touch with her when you went to Paris?'

'We did meet up now and again, yes; just for coffee or whatever. She was teaching near the place de la République, I think, and I was south of the river. She came to my flat a couple of times but she never invited me back to hers. It was somewhere near her school, if I remember rightly.'

'When was the last time you saw her?'

'Just after the Nazis invaded Paris. The time I went to her school to see if she was alright. I waited until classes had finished and we went to a café opposite.'

Again, Sophie paused.

'She didn't look at all well. Of course, it was the war, everything was in turmoil, people were fearful. But I couldn't help feeling there was something more at stake. She said she couldn't stay long, and didn't tell me anything, but kept looking around nervously and then suddenly upped and left.'

She took a large sip of cognac.

'But I'll never forget the look on her face.'

For the remaining couple of days at his grandparents' house, Steff saw things in a new light, something he had vaguely sensed but had not been able to express. There was tension there. He longed to ask his mother some questions in the light of what Sophie had said, but he knew it would be useless. She'd said the matter was closed. He would have to leave it there. For now.

5

Steff passed his A levels with flying colours. He'd knuckled down to his studies and it turned out that his time with Caro and her family did indeed help him, even though when he'd said that to his mother it was just because it sounded good. Being immersed in the language every day gave him a wider scope than the dialogue with his mother as he'd grown up. Caro loved literature, both French and English, and their many chats while they were driving around Picardy were useful for both subjects.

Griff and Scooby had stayed on at school too, but had done science subjects so their paths hardly crossed. When they did, they would chat politely but briefly. It was as if the three recognised tacitly that the railway days were over. It was still there, in the attic. Steff's teenage cousins, at the suggestion of his father, occasionally came to play with it, under supervision. And Steff found himself enjoying these afternoons more than he expected. A couple of times he toyed with the idea of seeing if the Grooby would be interested in coming over, for old times' sakes it were. But he dismissed the thought almost as soon as it came to him. Let those days remain the joyous times they were, he reasoned, rather than try to resuscitate them.

Fitz had left school as soon as he could, and had got a job in the timber yard, where they had bought the wood for the railway years ago, as it now seemed. He caught sight of him around town a couple of times but for reasons he couldn't have articulated didn't want to make contact with him. There came a Saturday morning when they almost bumped into each other turning a street corner from opposite directions. Fitz greeted him with one of his wide grins.

'Orright? What you up to?'

'Not much. Schoolwork and such.'

''Spose someone's got to do it. Fancy a pint sometime? Catch up?'

Steff felt he couldn't refuse, and agreed, thinking nothing would come of it. But Fitz got in touch with him a couple of weeks later and they did meet at one o'clock in The Cambrian Arms where his mother was behind the bar. She was a female version of Fitz, sharp-witted and no-nonsense. Steff was hungry and had a Cornish pasty in mind.

'Got anything hot?' he asked as she poured their pints.

'Well, how about Elaine here?' she said, nodding over her shoulder at the young, rather prim-looking barmaid and letting out a peal of smokey laughter. Elaine blushed but he detected a sneaky, cheeky grin.

It was a companionable enough hour or two they spent together. Fitz could still make him laugh. But on

parting, even though they agreed to do it again so
of them somehow knew it wouldn't happen.

Steff had set his sights on university in London, which
he'd come to think of as a magical place, where anything
could happen. His childhood and youth in Aberystwyth
had been happy enough, yet there was sometimes a feeling
of loneliness, and occasionally a certain melancholy would
descend on him, especially on a grey Sunday afternoon
when everything was closed. Seaside towns are meant to
be happy places, the motion of the waves consoling, but
on winter days the view across the bay could be bleak and
somehow claustrophobic in contrast to the customary
sense of space. He was eager to leave.

His father was encouraging, but his mother wasn't
best pleased.

'Do you have to go to the other side of the country?'
she said. 'I'm sure they have universities nearer home.'

They were walking along the beach at Borth.

'Maman, it's not exactly the end of the world. I could
be going to Aberdeen, or abroad. That's what you did
when you were not much older than me.'

He could tell as soon as the words were out of his
mouth that it wasn't a nice thing to say. He thought he
heard a little groan and she looked out to sea. The matter
was closed. He'd won, but it wasn't a good feeling.

His first choice was to study European Studies and
Linguistics at the prestigious School of International
Affairs in Malet Street. He liked the sound of it because
he could take modules in politics, history and philosophy.
He supposed the course would be sought after, and was

surprised when he got an interview. He was even more surprised at the form it took: three informal chats with lecturers one after the other. The strangest of all was with Wilfred Tonge who taught philosophy and was without doubt the most urbane person he'd ever clapped eyes on. He leant back in his chair, feet on his desk, and clasped the tips of his fingers together as if he was going to ask him the most taxing of questions.

'Do you like pictures?'

Steff was thrown off his stride and mumbled that there was only one picture house in his town and they didn't show very good films.

'No, no, my dear boy. Art! Do you like Art?'

Steff didn't have much to say about that either, and was convinced he'd ruined his chances. He'd have to settle for Bristol. So it was yet another surprise when he tore open the envelope containing his letter of acceptance.

By this time Steff thought of himself as fairly worldly, knowing Paris and all. But landing in London was an eye-opener to say the least, an education in itself. He shared a room at the top of a hall of residence off Southampton Row – a terrace of Victorian houses knocked into one. It could barely contain three beds, three chests of drawers, a sink and a gas meter for the fire. His two roommates were both from the North of England, one reading International Relations and the other Philosophy. The one from Halifax, Paul, had rows of LPs filling a bookshelf on the wall, and, as Steff soon discovered that much of the chat in the bar in the basement was devoted to what music people liked, he took to listening to them when he was alone. His repertoire was woefully scant, and he knew instinctively that Edith Piaf and male voice choirs would not cut any ice with this with-it lot. When he was asked one night in the bar for his favourite music, he said, with not much confidence, 'I quite like Soul Mix.'

He could tell from their reaction that he had said something which puzzled them. One or two of their circle nodded sagely. It was as if some were asking themselves if he could be that stupid, whereas others thought he was onto something new, a group they'd never heard of. Of course, when he had a chance to check the album again he saw the list of various groups written on the sleeve. It was a compilation.

In College, too, there was something new to learn everyday, and not just in the lecture rooms. There were students from all around the world, from America, Israel and a Cape Coloured from South Africa. In classes he particularly enjoyed learning about the Second World War, and France's role in it. It was just before it that his mother had moved to London, and just after that his aunt had, to all intents and purposes, disappeared. He was staggered by the number of Jews who were deported from Paris, and indeed the whole of the country, even so-called Free France. His mother had never spoken a word about this, and it puzzled him. She probably wouldn't have known, he told himself. It happened before she left for London. Should he ask her? She was so touchy about that period of her life. He would have to pick his moment.

Meanwhile he plucked up the nerve and went up to his politics lecturer, Madame Perriolat, after a morning class. She was packing up her things in her scruffy leather bag and looked at him rather impatiently, he thought, when he said, 'Excuse me, Madame,' and felt his courage fail him.

'Yes?' she said when he remained silent.

'Could I ask you a question?'

'By all means,' and, when there was another pause, 'Well, what is it?'

He managed to take control of himself and asked her what was generally known about what was happening in Paris in 1942 when Jews were rounded up and sent to the death camps. Her answer surprised him.

'Virtually nothing at all. Unless people lived in Jewish areas or actually witnessed them being taken away, that is.'

She slung her bag over a shoulder and started making for the door. Steff thought that would be it. But she looked back at him.

'It's an interesting question with a complicated answer. Look, I'm starving. Do you want to get a bite to eat and we can chat about it?'

Steff felt flattered, and himself blush. His lecturer was quite young and attractive, with flaming red hair and a somewhat sardonic grin. There was speculation in the class about whether she was French or British, as her accent sounded British generally but not localised – it didn't seem to come from somewhere.

She suggested they go to Rizzoli's, round the corner in Torrington Place. He'd been there once or twice and liked it – an Italian café run by what seemed to be a family of a small elderly woman, an equally small young woman, and a tall young man. They all had the same look.

Mme Perriolat was clearly a regular and was greeted warmly. She ordered minestrone, bread roll and a glass of red wine as she made her way to an empty booth. Steff ordered the same with a nod and a smile.

She took up her narrative straightaway.

'It's murky because nothing was reported about the round-ups in the press or on the radio. Journalism, as they say, is the first draft of history. In this case there was no such draft. So people had to rely on hearsay. The raids were at dawn, so there wouldn't have been many people around. Some locals might have heard rumours but they probably didn't know whether to believe them or not. And in fact nothing much has been written about it ever since.'

'You mean for more than twenty years?'

'That's right. It seems a veil of official secrecy has shrouded the whole subject. When I was teaching in Paris I was amazed that nothing was said about the French authorities' complicity in the deportations. I questioned it, but was told that it was not part of the curriculum. You know the old saying that every pupil in France is reading the same word in the same book at the same time? Thanks to Napoleon. Well, there's some truth in it. It's only now that journalists and writers are beginning to revisit the whole sorry affair. And most people still believe that it was all the Nazis' doing, that the French police had nothing to do with it. There's a plaque going up in a school playground where some of the Jews were first taken. There's already some controversy about it, as it blames the Germans, no mention of the French *milice* – the military police. But there was a vicious and vociferous growth in antisemitism in France before the war too. It had been bubbling along ever since the Dreyfus affair – remember, we touched on it in class?'

'Yes, the Jewish major in the French army who was convicted of selling state secrets to the Germans in the 1890s and sent to Devil's Island in French Guiana.'

'My, my,' said Mme Perriolat. 'It's heartening to know that at least someone has been listening to me droning on. That's right – years later he was exonerated and re-instated when it was proved that the Army forged evidence and protected the real culprit. For his supporters it became the ultimate symbol of miscarriage of justice and antisemitism. But his detractors, mainly the Catholic right wing, it has to be said, refused to believe in his innocence. The affair divided and polarised France.'

She told him about a book that she'd heard on the grapevine was coming out soon which documented the round-ups and deportations. She offered to try to find out more about it and let him know the details and when it was published. She asked him why he was so interested. He pondered for a moment whether to mention the disappearance of his aunt, and whether indeed it was relevant. Until this moment he hadn't linked the two events in his mind. But she'd been open and honest with him and so he decided to tell her.

'And now a question for you. Is your family Jewish?'

'Uh…no. No, I'm pretty sure they're not. My mother came from a French catholic family and my father's Welsh and his family is Wesleyan.'

'Hmm. Well, it's as well to be sure if you're going to pursue your investigation into your aunt's disappearance.'

It was the first time he'd heard anyone express it so formally, but he realised in a flash that that was what he wanted to do. And now, in his newfound spirit of enquiry, something she had said struck him as potentially interesting. He'd never been satisfied by his mother's assertion that the family had been to the Lycée Émile Zola where his aunt had taught and drawn a blank. It was a long shot, but he asked Mme Perriolat where she taught in Paris.

'In Enghien-les-bains, in the north of the city.'

Steff knew roughly where it was, on the railway line between St Lazare and Pontoise, but he could see no connection to his family.

She got up abruptly, as was her style, gathered her things rather clumsily and said goodbye. As she made her way towards the door, she called back over her shoulder, 'Don't call me Madame,' and as she opened the door, 'It's Anne.'

In the third year of the course students were expected to work or study in the country of the language they were majoring in. Steff had set his heart on Paris, but didn't want to have to stay with his grandparents. He was advised by his tutor George Kenny that a placement as *assistant d'Anglais* in a Parisian lycée was a tall order and something of a lottery. It was hugely competitive and you couldn't specify where you wanted to go. If you didn't get a placement you were more or less left to fend for yourself. He filled in the forms putting his first preference as English assistant at a school in Paris and spent several nervous weeks waiting for the decision. At one point it crossed his mind that it would be fantastic if he got a place at his aunt's old school, but tried to dismiss it immediately – surely it would be too much to expect. The most he could hope for was that, if he did get a place, it wouldn't be anywhere near Conflans, so he could tell his grandparents that it would be too far to commute.

When the offer came, it exceeded all his expectations. It was in Villeneuve-sous-Sénart, south of Paris. It was a *lycée expérimental,* which, Steff discovered, was something of a flagship school and as such would be well funded and have certain freedoms to depart from the national curriculum in a bid to find new and creative ways to learn. Furthermore, there was accommodation in the school for the four assistants – English, German, Russian and Chinese. His grandparents would have no reason, he thought, to complain that he would not be going to stay with them.

His grandmother found one though.

'Well of course, we expected you to come to stay with us,' she said when he phoned to tell her. 'You're family, after all.'

He tried in vain to explain that he was expected to live in, with the three other assistants. It was part of being *expérimental* and he'd thought somehow that she would

58

be impressed but she didn't seem to get it at all. *Tant pis*, he thought.

The only other one of his classmates who got a place in a lycée was his friend Pete, who got posted to Argenteuil, the other side of Paris. They got the boat train from Victoria together and spent three days on a course in the Sorbonne, cooped up in a somewhat dingy hotel nearby sharing four to a room with a guy from Glasgow and one from Norfolk. Then they went their separate ways, Steff to the Gare de Lyon to get the train to Villeneuve with a swelling sense of adventure.

6

The iron gates of the lycée de Villeneuve-sous-Sénart looked as if they were the entrance to a chateau, and indeed further up the tree-lined avenue there was a rather grand *manoir* style house, which turned out to be the headmaster's residence.

He'd been told to meet a Madame Baxter at the main entrance. He wondered whether she'd be English, or British, and whether they'd picked her out specially to meet the English assistant. The trouble was, it was far from evident where the main entrance was. Through the trees he caught glimpses of the school buildings: dating from the thirties, he would have said, and looking somehow more Germanic than Gallic. They were two storeys, or rather three for the red-tiled roofs were lined with dormer windows. He took a path to the left towards the buildings but as he approached he could see no doors save a small side one which couldn't possibly be the main entrance. A man was hoeing a flower bed so he asked him. It turned out the main entrance was not through the gate he'd just come through but another one the other side of the park. Here there was a modern looking grill with a series of glassed doors opposite. Standing there was a woman in her late forties, he guessed. It gave him quite a shock. She was the dead spit of Scooby's mother. She had a Welsh look about her, although he couldn't have described what that look was. Maybe something to do with high cheek bones and a small mouth.

She addressed him in English: a fluent, unaccented English but he could somehow tell it was not her mother tongue. She said she'd show him to the assistants' quarters in another building. As they walked through the trees he found that she was an English teacher who'd married an Englishman and spent some time in the Home Counties teaching there. He got the impression that she liked taking the English assistants under her wing.

Mme Baxter ushered him up a few steps onto the door of a separate building, in the same style as the rest, with a sand-coloured facade.

'The canteens are on the ground floor,' she said, 'one for the staff and one for the pupils. On the first floor there are the assistants' rooms, bathrooms, and a little foyer with a TV. And the Moulecs live there too – they're the caretakers, a married couple, who've been here for years. Probably longer than anyone else. Madame Moulec likes looking after the assistants.' There was a twinkle in her eye. She led him upstairs, walked half way down a long corridor, all painted in institutional cream, and knocked on a door. It was opened almost immediately by a woman with curly grey hair, a blue overall and a huge smile.

Mme Baxter switched to French and introduced him. Mme Moulec had a strong Breton accent and a way of giving slight deferential bobs when someone spoke to her. She explained that his room was next door, shuffled towards it and unlocked the door. She called him Monsieur Lewis, pronounced Louise. He felt Mme Baxter eyeing him to see if he was following the French and raised her eyebrows when she heard his replies.

'There,' said Mme Moulec, waving her hand inwards. They let him go in and explore. There was a little hallway with shelves, a rail and hangers. The room itself was quite small with a single bed, a desk by the window, a table with a hotplate and some utensils on a shelf above, and a cupboard which opened up to reveal a washbasin. It was basic but Steff thought it had everything he needed.

He was then shown the foyer, a similar size with soft chairs and a small TV. 'This is for all the assistants, said Mme Baxter, 'so you can get to know each other. I think the others are arriving in a day or two. Their rooms are further down the corridor, beyond the bathrooms and shower rooms.'

Mme Baxter looked at him closely.

'You didn't learn your French at school, did you?' She'd reverted to English, and clearly liked talking in the language.

'Well, my mother's French. Father's Welsh.'

'Ah, that explains it. You can't tell you're not French because you speak the language so fluently without a foreign accent. But because you don't have a local or regional one either it's impossible to work out where you're from.'

'It's the same with your English.'

They both laughed, realising they were going to get on. Steff liked her directness.

'Well, you should have no problem here. Some of the ones they send over can be a little…,'she searched for the word, '…helpless, shall we say.'

She showed him around the school, some of the classrooms where he'd be teaching, and gave him his timetable. It was Friday afternoon, and his lessons started the next Tuesday. She said she'd do the first lesson with him.

'Now, I'll leave you to settle in.'

Over the next couple of days the other assistants arrived: Monsieur Zhen wore a Mao suit and was most polite and affable. He spoke no French or English and seemed to have two stock responses to anything anyone said. One was to say 'Oooh,' with a slight frown of concern, and the other was to give a little giggle. Steff wondered how he was going to manage in France. Ingrid from West Berlin was typical of her nation, thought Steff – tall with long dark blond hair. Valentina of the Soviet Union was middle-aged, a little frumpy and wore a surly expression. Steff took against her when they gathered briefly in the foyer on the Sunday evening. As soon as M Zhen left, Valentina laid into him and indeed the whole Chinese race.

'You can't trust him,' she pronounced in English. 'Those slitty eyes – you can never tell what they're thinking.'

'Oh, come on, Valentina, you've only just met him,' said Ingrid in her German's fluent English. 'You can't just attack a whole nation like that.'

Valentina upped and left.

Steff took an immediate shine to Ingrid. She had a warm smile and a silky voice. She was easy in her skin. He admired the way she'd stood up to Valentina. Left alone in the foyer, they chatted late into the evening, drinking the wine Steff had brought and delighting in finding common ground. He loved her voice and the way she spoke – so different from the war films which had given him his conception of Germany and Germans. He found young Germans in general intriguing – they seemed normal, nice people and so it puzzled him how they could have emerged from their recent history. He enjoyed finding out more about her country and her. When it came time to say goodnight, they did so quite politely. But when he caught her eyes, so shining, almost asking him to come with her, he had to look away. It was only afterwards that he forced himself to ask why: why did he reject her silent invitation? He settled down to an unsettled sleep. He'd had a few affairs, although that seemed too grand and euphemistic a term for his sexual encounters thus far. Nothing disastrous, but nothing worth writing home about either, as if the thought would even occur to him about telling his parents about such matters. No, it was because he felt Ingrid was beyond him: a couple of years older, a couple of inches taller, a sophisticated world away from what he knew. What could she possibly see in him?

Steff looked forward to his first lesson on the Tuesday and did not feel nervous, especially as Mme Baxter would be sitting in on it. He'd brought some material with him, including a sheet of the lyrics of *Penny Lane* which he thought they could translate together. Mme Baxter told him he could go and get copies at an office called *Documentation*. When he did so, the bulky no-nonsense woman at the counter snapped, 'On whose authority?'

'Well, my own, I suppose. I'm the English assistant.'

'The English assistant? You don't look old enough. And you don't sound English.'

He knew he looked young for his age, and as there were no school uniforms in the lycée, which he found strange, he realised he could easily be mistaken for a pupil.

'I've just arrived. It's for a session with Première. Fifteen copies please.'

She gave a resigned shrug, fairly snatched his paper from him and made the copies.

Mme Baxter was waiting for him in the classroom along with most of the students wearing expectant looks. A couple looked as if they were ready to make mischief. On the whole they were polite and engaged apart from a bit of sniggering at the back, which Mme Baxter stifled with a look. The song went down quite well, apart from a comment he heard from one guy with long, greasy hair: '*Les Beatles, c'est des chansons maman et papa*' (The Beatles' songs are for Mum and Dad). He came to regret his choice though when it came to the phrase 'fish and finger pie.' He didn't know how to explain fish fingers (Mme Baxter supplied *petits poissons panés*), let alone why they said fish *and* finger pie. He didn't understand it himself.

'*Une tarte aux doigts et poissons panés*?' asked an incredulous girl in the front row. Mme Baxter shot him an inquisitive glance.

'It's a play on words,' he said in English, as that's what he was supposed to do, and attempted to elaborate. The whole class looked even more confused.

'It's sort of surreal,' he said weakly. When they'd finished the translation he asked them what it told them about Liverpool, its people and history, and the background of the group. This seemed to work well, and they asked questions with varying degrees of fluency.

The class filed out chatting with smiles on their faces, which Steff took as a good sign.

'Well done,' said Mme Baxter. 'You'll be fine. Now let's go and get some lunch.'

Steff stopped off at the staff toilet she'd pointed out to him. As he was washing his hands, a female teacher came in (another unfamiliar custom), flung her arm towards the door and shouted, 'Get out!'

He began to mumble a protest but she repeated her command more forcefully, adding 'You know you're not supposed to be here.'

'I'm the English assistant,' he shouted.

She squinted at him, looking sceptical, but apologised and ducked into a cubicle.

In the canteen, Mme Baxter found some other English teachers sitting at a large round table. They were welcoming and friendly, and the conversation was in English.

'His mother's French and he's fluent,' she said.

'That'll come in handy,' said a petite feisty woman. 'But remember you're here so they can hear English and speak it.'

'Of course,' said Steff.

'"When we are born we cry that we are come to this great stage of fools,"' said a dapper man with a flourish of his right arm, apropos of nothing it seemed. Steff thought it sounded like a Shakespeare quote, and came to learn that it was the teacher's habit.

He watched carefully to see what they would order for lunch and most of them went for the three course option – pâté, chicken chasseur, cheese and a half bottle of wine, all for a few francs, so he followed suit.

For the rest of the week's classes he flew solo and they went off as well as he could have hoped. It was to his advantage, he reasoned, that the pupils were quite keen to learn English. He taught the top three years: Seconde, Première and Terminale – three different groups in each.

On the Wednesday evening, he and Ingrid went out to explore the town. Villeneuve-sous-Sénart was a sleepy little suburb which seemed to shut up around nine in the evening. They found a café that was still open and had a couple of beers and a sandwich. Pete had sent him a postcard saying he and some others were meeting in Paris on Friday night, at a place called Polly Maggoo's on the Left Bank. He asked Ingrid if she'd like to go and she said, 'With great pleasure.' Her English was very good if a bit formal at times.

They found it easily enough and approved of it wholeheartedly: the benches were old metro seats and the tables had old maps of Paris under glass. On the side wall there was what looked like a huge black and red film poster featuring a striking woman's face framed in black hair with the title *Qui êtes-vous Polly Maggoo*? Steff had never heard of it – he'd have to check it out. At a table towards the back they found Pete, the Glaswegian Duncan they'd shared a room with for the induction course, and a couple of young women, also English assistants, whom Duncan knew. They shuffled up to let Steff and Ingrid in, and there they stayed until the early hours, apart from the odd visit to the loos. They were the only real downside of the place: two grimy cubicles behind dilapidated saloon doors tethered with loops of string. After a couple of drinks, it didn't seem to matter.

The six hit it off immediately and it was a convivial evening. They compared notes on their first teaching week, and swapped ideas of what worked well in class. It became clear to Steff (and to Ingrid too judging by the looks they exchanged) that their lycée was in a league of its own – the others had only one *assistant*.

Ingrid and Steff didn't notice the time slipping by and had to run for the last train to Villeneuve. As they walked towards the door of his room, he badly wanted to ask her in for coffee…or something. And indeed he sensed her slowing her pace as they approached. But all he could manage was, 'Well, I guess it's goodnight.' She smiled and said, 'Well, I guess it is,' and give him a lingering kiss on the cheek. 'Thanks for a lovely evening.'

Too late, he held out his arm as if to pull her back but she was already striding down the corridor towards her room. He entered his, thumped his fist against the wall, and then shook it as if to dispel the hurt. It didn't work.

In the lesson with the Seconde the following week, he tried a tip he'd got from Duncan: lateral thinking conundrums. They'd tried out a few in Polly Maggoo's. It was a bigger class, around twenty.

'A man gets up in the morning, opens the curtains in his bedroom, and sees a church spire,' he said. 'The next morning, he gets up, opens the curtains, and there's no church spire. Why?'

There were some puzzled looks, and not just because they didn't know why. Tempted as he was just to translate into the French, he felt honour bound to keep to English. He found himself miming it: lying on the front desks with his eyes closed, opening them and stretching (repeating 'get up') and going over to the window and making curtain-opening swishes ('open the curtains'). Then he said 'church,' which they seemed to understand, and then made a large triangle shape on top. He could see light bulbs going on. He did the whole thing again, in English, and this time he waved his hands across each other to signal 'no spire.' They got it, and asked some good questions albeit in halting English.

'The church spire was...,' and, not knowing the English for demolish, the boy made an explosion sound and then made a tumbling down motion with his hands.

Steff shook his head.

'He was in another room?'

'No, same room.'

And so it went on. In the end they give up, one

pupil saying, 'we give our tongues to the cat,' – a direct translation of a French idiom for giving up on a puzzle. It made him think of something his Welsh grandmother used to say when he didn't speak up: 'Has the cat got your tongue?' Could they possibly be related? So in the end he told them: 'He was on a boat.'

It took a while for the penny to drop, but then there were a few aahs, with a couple of pupils explaining it to their neighbours. He could tell it was a hit, and they wanted more. After two others, they said they wanted to do one for him. 'OK, good,' he said, but they told him he'd have to go out of the room when they prepared.

So he did.

It seemed at first a reasonable and intriguing request, but as he waited outside the door and heard desks and chairs being moved around he began to feel foolish. What if Mme Baxter or indeed any other teacher came along? What would he say? And what on earth were they doing?

He was just thinking he should go back in and see when a small head popped around the door and said, 'You come now, sir.'

Desks had been pushed in front of the back wall and on top of them in the middle were two others, behind which sat one pupil looking self-important. In front of that row one desk had been placed to the left and one to the right, in front of which sat two other pupils, facing the wall and the row of desks. It was unmistakably a courtroom. Chairs had been arranged to form a dock, in which stood a boy wearing a scruffy coat and a sullen look. He had to hand it to them for their imagination and creativity, but he shuddered to think what was in store, or what anyone would make of it if they happened to walk by.

To their credit, they did their best to conduct the trial in English, asking him for translations from the French from time to time. In due course the judge banged the blackboard rubber on his desk and looked at the accused. 'You are a bad teacher,' he said. 'You hit the boy.' Steff was sure he hadn't heard the accused enter a plea of guilty or otherwise. He conceded though that he could hardly expect them to follow court procedure to the letter.

The judge then looked at him. 'How do you say *la peine de mort*?' Steff hesitated a moment, then felt he had to say 'the death sentence.'

'I condame you to the dess sentence.' he said with another bang of the rubber. Two boys came and led him struggling away, to the applause of the rest of the class sitting in a semi-circle around the courtroom set.

They gathered around him and asked him what it was about. It was far from what he thought of as lateral thinking but the matter was pretty obvious.

'A teacher hit a boy.'

'Yes,' said the judge, who seemed to be something of the class ringleader and whom Steff thought must have masterminded the trial. 'A teacher at our school, Monsieur Dubois.' It had happened a couple of years before, in their class. M Dubois was unpopular, scruffy and cruel. He'd been dismissed from the school, but no-one could tell him what happened to him after that.

'Still,' said Steff, 'the death sentence was a little harsh.'

He told them to move the desks back as noiselessly as they could and while they did so, got them to repeat key phrases. At least they must have learnt something, he thought.

Life at the lycée fell into a comfortable pattern. Steff enjoyed the lessons and he seemed to have gained the trust of the pupils – most of them at least. He suspected that they had him down as an eccentric, which would fit into their perception of the English, as they saw it. He knew it was wrong to laugh at their mistakes, so he could find himself spluttering and coughing when he tried to stifle laughter. When they wanted to know about the British monarchy, he asked who knew the name of the Queen's husband.

'Ze duck of Edinbourg,' said a boy in the front. Steff imagined a duck in a top hat waddling behind his wife and failed to suppress a laugh. But when he explained, they found it funny too. A tall boy in Terminale sidled up to him after their afternoon class and asked him if he could have a word. It turned out that his mother was keen to improve her English but was sensitive and worried that people would laugh at her when she spoke it. She'd need to be treated kindly, said the boy. Steff agreed to go to their house on Wednesday afternoons when there were no classes. They lived the other side of the forest, and he enjoyed the walk. The mother was a nice, shy women. They sat in the kitchen and chatted in simple English. When she revealed that 'my best friend is a cooker,' Steff had to bite his cheeks. No harm was done, and they continued the conversation classes for the rest of the school year. Her English improved impressively.

Three or four pupils asked for private lessons. They came to his room after class. One of them, quite a studious fellow, said he wanted to know more about *Martaluterka*, which they were studying for their brevet, the equivalent of O levels. Even with his familiarity of French pronunciation, it took Steff a couple of moments to realise he was talking about Martin Luther King.

The teachers assured him that he was proving popular and his classes were effective. One of them, Mme Giraud, asked if he'd give her son Didier conversation classes. Steff thought this a little strange, given that his mother was an English teacher, but he went along with it. She said to come on Saturday mornings and he could stay to lunch.

Didier was a rather odd gangly young man of about twenty or so. Steff found the sessions a little hard-going because he didn't seem to have any interests and they had little in common. He was studying Engineering, for which he probably needed English, but didn't seem to enjoy their time together particularly. He would disappear after lunch – sometimes before it – and Steff and Mme Giraud would chat over coffee. In due course she took him into her confidence.

'I'm a bit worried about Didier. He doesn't seem to have any friends,' she said. 'And he spends a lot of his time washing his hands.'

Steff didn't know how to respond to this, or what to do about it.

'Maybe he should see a doctor?'

'He refuses to go. He doesn't communicate very much, but it seems there's something on his mind.'

'Perhaps it'll work itself out,' said Steff.

'I hope so. He seems to like you coming here. He hasn't said anything to you, has he? About any worries, I mean.'

'No, nothing at all. He doesn't open up much. And I've got the impression that he doesn't do these lessons very willingly.'

'That's just his way. I'm not putting any pressure on him, believe me. It wouldn't work if I did. I'm just worried that there's some guilty secret he's harbouring. All that hand-wringing. I just want him to know that whatever it is, he'd feel better if he talked about it. Not to me necessarily – maybe you? A problem shared and all that.'

'Well, I don't know how I can help,' said Steff, 'but I'm there if he wants to talk.'

The sessions continued, and over time Steff began to think Didier was deriving some benefit from them, and seemed to relax a little. After one Saturday lunch Steff suggested they go for a couple of beers in the Café de la Gare. Didier didn't exactly jump at the chance, but went along with it. Steff had thought he might come out of his shell, but although he made desultory conversation, he didn't reveal anything about himself. Steff pondered how he could encourage him to talk, but he couldn't find a way. He told him about the Tante, how his family closed ranks and their mouths about her, so that it felt like a secret he wasn't in on. For a moment or two an unaccustomed glint came into Didier's eyes: he was intrigued. But the look went as soon as it had come, and shortly after he offered to drive Steff back to the school. Steff took this as a good sign and the next week invited him to go into Paris one evening to meet his friends. Didier thanked him politely and said he'd think about it. But nothing came of it. The next Saturday he was in a bad mood and was virtually monosyllabic. Maybe Steff had tried to get too close.

The extra money from the private lessons came in handy, and Steff was able to enjoy a good social life in a way that he hadn't in London. Friday nights at Polly Maggoo's became a regular fixture with Pete and the gang, for Ingrid too. Mr Zhen went around with a small group of his similarly clad compatriots, and Valentina kept herself very much to herself and they saw very little of her.

He and Ingrid went out together often, exploring Paris. Mme Baxter took her under her wing too, inviting them to dinner, taking them to the Basilica of St Denis to see the tombs of the kings of France, and to the chateaux of the Loire. The couple became close, but their relationship didn't seem to progress beyond a chaste goodnight kiss. Steff came to think that she wanted more, as indeed did he. The last time they went back to their rooms after a night out, she stroked his cheek with the back of her hand. Was she waiting for him to make a move, inviting him almost? Somehow he couldn't bring himself to, and didn't really understand why. He was aware that he didn't want to jeopardise what they had, and worried what would happen if it was the wrong move. Then after a a couple of months in Villeneuve, Ingrid dropped a bombshell. Her boyfriend Gunter would be coming from Germany for a long weekend in a month or so. She had never mentioned him before. She told him quite casually as if no explanation were needed given the closeness they'd developed together – it seemed she just wanted friendship, companionship after all. Steff retired hurt and realised that his preoccupation with her had taken up much time and energy. He wanted to continue their socialising and so they did. He tried hard though to step back mentally from any hopes for the future. As a distraction he decided he should face up to something he'd been putting off for too long – going to see his grandparents in Conflans. At least there would be the consolation of going to see Rita and Bob next door for an evening (or two). He'd have to negotiate that quite carefully, and now he had some more questions to ask his grandparents about the disappearance of his aunt. It wasn't going to be easy.

7

Steff convinced himself that he didn't deliberately choose the weekend of Gunter's visit to go to Conflans, but that it just worked out that way. In his mind's eye he already saw him as tall, fair and athletic – a perfect match for Ingrid: the golden couple. How could he compete? It was with a rather heavy heart that he got the train from Saint Lazare on a Thursday night. His grandmother had not been gracious when he phoned to say he would like to come: why had he left it so long? They'd been looking forward to seeing him. He was ready for that one. He'd had to settle in to his work, preparing for lessons and so on. He told her he'd also managed to sign up for a one-year arts course at the Sorbonne, called a DEUG, designed for students who it was felt needed extra tuition between the *baccalauréat* (the equivalent of A levels) and their degree. He hoped it would impress her, although it was difficult to work out what exactly did impress her. And it wasn't a lie, but he'd attended only three sessions. They were rather useless, he decided. A handful or two of students dotted around one of the huge old semi-circular lecture halls, called amphitheatres, with rows of hard wooden seats, almost like choir stalls. The lecturer would come in, sit at the tribune in the front, and blether on for an hour about the book they should have read for that week. No-one spoke to him, or to each other it seemed. By the end of the third session he'd had enough, and decided he would rather be with Ingrid.

When he rang Rita she immediately invited him to dinner on the Saturday night. 'That would be great,' said Steff, 'but it won't go down well. I'll have to think of an excuse.'

Rita came to the rescue. 'Tell her you need help with your lessons,' she said. 'Bob and I are going to help you.'

'Great idea,' said Steff. 'And it's not wholly untrue. Any help gratefully received.'

It was indeed a white lie, or rather a greyish one. He had a ten thousand word thesis to write in French in his final year, and he was supposed to study for it in his year abroad, when he could make use of local source material. He'd chosen the actor Jean Gabin. He'd seen the film *La Bête Humaine*, an adaptation of the Zola novel. Gabin was a train driver based in St Lazare station, so of course Steff was captivated, even though it was an old black and white film from the 1930s. But when he'd gone to get his subject approved, George Kenny had his doubts.

'Hmm. It's supposed to be an academic subject. I'm not sure a film actor will cut it.'

Steff wondered how much Kenny knew about Gabin.

He'd done some research, as it had crossed his mind that it might be a hard sell.

'Well he's one of the foremost actors in France. He's also a singer of chansons, about the lives of ordinary working people.'

'Tell you what,' said Kenny, puffing on his pipe, 'find out a bit more and convince me.'

Steff went to the university library in Senate House, the huge Stalinist-looking building on Malet Street, but could find next to no biographical material about him, which he thought would help his cause but hinder its execution. He tried the Institut Français in South Kensington and here there were many cuttings about his life and work. He went back to see Kenny.

'He refused to stay in Paris after the German occupation. He'd met Marlene Dietrich there and they both went to Hollywood, where they had an affair and she taught him English. In fact the FBI suspected they were working on a secret code to help the Vichy regime against the Nazis. But American life didn't suit him and he returned to fight with de Gaulle's Free French against the collaborators. He was awarded the *Croix de Guerre*. So there is a historical and political aspect,' said Steff, 'as well as an artistic and, well, glamorous one.'

'Well done,' said Kenny. 'That's some good research to start with. Gabin is approved. But find a theme.'

'That's great,' said Steff. 'Thanks.'

'You can go to the Cinématèque Française in the Palais de Chaillot. They have the largest film archive in the world, not just films themselves but scripts and books.'

So although there was literature to research, including the plight of cinema and the arts under the Nazi

Occupation, the bulk of his study in Paris consisted, to his great satisfaction, of watching films and reading scripts.

He'd got a late train to Conflans so it was about ten thirty when he arrived at the house. His grandmother seemed genuinely pleased to see him, and even cracked a weak smile as she kissed and hugged him. His grandfather was nowhere to be seen – in bed, presumably, but no information was forthcoming.

'I've kept you some dinner,' she said, bearing a casserole with two kitchen gloves and placing it on a trivet in the centre of the table. 'I know you must be hungry.'

Steff knew it was useless to protest that he'd had a substantial lunch in the canteen and a ham and cheese baguette he'd picked up at the station. So he had to sit and force it down, fortunately with some wine from the carafe she placed next to him, and she sat opposite and watched him. He was thinking about the questions he had for his grandparents: what they knew about Nazi-occupied Paris and, trickiest of all, whether there was any Jewishness in the family. It would be no good broaching the subject while they were at the table – meals there were quite a quiet affair with just small talk about the weather, plans for the next day and so forth.

He found his grandfather in his shed the next morning, tinkering with a bit of electronic equipment. Even though he was fairly taciturn, Steff thought it would somehow be easier to get information from him than his grandmother. He started off gently, asking about his Papie's childhood.

'Born and raised in Achères, over the river,' he said, concentrating on filing a part of the motor and holding it up to the light for inspection.

'Is that where your family's from?'

'Going back as far back as I can tell.'

'Is that where Mamie is from?'

'Next village.'

'How did you meet her?'

Steff was gaining confidence in this question and answer session. As brief as the responses were, his grandfather didn't seem to mind supplying the information, as long as he didn't have to look his grandson in the eye.

'At the village dance, in the square.'

'Where did you get married? In the local church?'

'Of course.'

'Was it a Catholic service?'

Here, for the first time, he shot his grandson a glance with a frown. Steff read it as more of curiosity than annoyance.

'Of course,' he said again.

'So both your families were staunch Catholics?'

Papie nodded.

Steff switched tack and asked him about the war and how it affected them. The old man seemed to relish relating this era which was clearly so fresh in his memory.

'Well, when war was declared there was panic. Women and children were packed off to the country to stay with relatives and on farms. But then by Christmas nothing had happened so they all came back. The *drôle de guerre*, they called it.'

The funny war, thought Steff. The phoney war in English. Maybe one was derived from the other.

'Your mother was in England and Céleste was teaching in Paris. She wouldn't leave.'

'And how much did you know about what was going on in Paris?'

His Papie reflected a moment, seeming to consider it an interesting question.

'Well, the press and radio were controlled by the Nazis so we couldn't rely on anything they said. There were rumours of course, but we couldn't know how true they were.'

'What kind of rumours?'

'About how the Jews were being treated, I suppose. They couldn't go out to public places. Of course we'd heard about the Nazis' attitude to them in the build up to the war.'

'And here in France, there was a lot of antisemitism too, wasn't there?'

Here his grandfather threw him another wary look.

'Well, yes, in lots of countries the Jews weren't popular. For one reason or another.'

Steff was struck by the word 'reason.'

'What we did know was that food was getting harder and harder to come by, and thousands of people were leaving for the country and the South. Some of our neighbours did.'

'So Tante Céleste could have left too.'

'We've told you that we had no idea what happened to her,' he said after a pause, and this time there was anger in his voice, which signalled that the interview was at an end. He'd gone too far.

Steff suspected that it had been the longest conversation his grandfather had had in quite a while. As he climbed up the steps back to the house, he thought he could probably rule out the possibility that his lecturer had raised in Rizzoli's café – that his aunt could have been a victim of the Nazis. And he now remembered that solitary postcard she'd sent after the war. His feeling strengthened that they didn't want to know what happened to her – or didn't want him to know.

The next evening with Rita and Bob couldn't have been more of a contrast to the stultifying climate at his grandparents'. Predictably his Mamie had not taken kindly to his news of their invitation. It was obvious she didn't approve of them, and muttered something about drunken parties and loud noise. As he walked over he took in deep, appreciative breaths – already the air seemed fresher. There was another couple there, drinking pastis and eating olives and salami: a science teacher at Bob's school, Henri and his wife Marie-Claude, so the conversation was in French. The party seemed already to be in full swing and they greeted him warmly.

'What's that music?' Steff asked Rita as she ushered him to the long wooden dining table in the kitchen.

'*Bei Mir Bist du Shein*. The Andrews Sisters,' she said, blowing out a cloud of smoke from her Disque Bleu.

'What language is that?'

'Yiddish,' she said without elaborating. He'd have to find more about that, he promised himself.

Henri was quite a comedian who kept them entertained. Bob mentioned a female colleague at work and Henri said, 'You mean the one with those wonderful...,' and rounded his hands in front of his chest. He must have caught his wife's eye and he ended with '...diplomas.'

They sat down to a sumptuous supper. For the main course Bob had made *coq au vin* – real *coq au vin* he said with heavy emphasis as Rita served it.

'He spent all morning going from shop to shop trying to find a *coq*, insisting that only a male of the species would do,' she said.

'Well, it's just wrong,' said Bob. 'The dish isn't *poulet au vin*, is it?'

'Mmm – it's marvellous,' said Henri after a taste. 'Much stronger and tastier than the female version.' He leered at his wife. 'Do you fancy *coq* from now on, kid?'

'Good luck with that,' said Marie-Claude. She had a dry sense of humour.

After dinner, the conversation and wine continued to flow. Rita asked him how the search for his aunt was going. He outlined his limited progress and said he was thinking of going to her lycée and seeing if they had any records of her. Did they think schools would hold such information? There was general agreement that, yes, normally they would.

'But that depends' said Henri. 'There was some bombing before the Germans marched in. And a lot of disorder afterwards. Records could have been lost. And who knows how many Jews were at the school – staff and pupils. Their records would have been destroyed for a start.'

Steff told them about the school on the avenue de la République.

'Oh, I know that school,' said Bob. 'I did a placement there when I was doing my teacher's training a few years after the war. It's an old building and I can't remember any sign of damage or disorder. Everything seemed well regulated.'

Right, thought Steff, that's my next step. Go to the school. Encouraged by the enthusiasm they'd shown, he went on to ask them what was now generally known about the war and specifically about the fate of the Jews.

'Interesting you should say that,' said Bob. 'There's been a bit of press coverage recently. I think it was after a book was published.'

Must be the book that his lecturer mentioned, thought Steff. He'd have to get hold of it. Another action plan.

'What's beginning to emerge are the details of the round-ups and deportation of Jews and, more importantly, the complicity of the French authorities. Everything that happened in Paris has traditionally been blamed on the Nazis, but now it turns out that there was a lot of collaboration from gangs like the *milice*, the military police formed to do a lot of the dirty work.'

'There was a great deal of antisemitism here too, long before the war,' said Rita. 'But that was all conveniently forgotten after the liberation and the full horror of the death camps started coming out. If you'd listened to the

French, every single one of them was in the resistance. That was their war record.'

There were solemn nods around the table, and a discussion about what was taught in schools – who decided what, and why. The teachers criticised the straight jacket of the national curriculum. Steff thought again how lucky he was to be teaching in an experimental school.

As fluent as Steff was in the language, he was realising there were a lot of references in their conversation that he just didn't get. After the other guests left, he asked Bob what he should read to get more in the swim of things.

'Ah, what all left-wing intellectuals read, of course.'

Steff couldn't tell if he was being serious or not. Probably not. Bob went on to suggest the satirical papers Charlie Hebdo and Le Canard Enchaîné, both in the radical and secular tradition. The latter, he said, was a bit like Private Eye, but there was nothing quite like Charlie Hebdo. Totally irreverent, it mocked all power and pomp with cartoons and jokes. Steff resolved to check it out. Bob also recommended singers such as Brel, Moustaki and Gréco. The phrase philosophical bohemianism was mentioned.

The evening flew by and before Steff knew it, it was past midnight. He had a key but feared he'd disturb the grandparents and the consequences would not be pleasant. Rita urged him to stay in a spare room. Yes, that would be better. He'd had quite a bit to drink and could picture himself staggering noisily up the stairs. He'd get up early and creep back in.

Of course that plan didn't work. He woke up late and rushed downstairs, said a quick goodbye to Rita and slunk in next door. His grandmother was standing by the kitchen sink. There was bread, croissants, jam and coffee on the table. She said nothing, but her silence and the look she gave him were reproof enough.

'Sorry, Mamie, it got late and they asked me to stay so I thought it would be better than coming back and disturbing you.'

He thought the explanation sounded reasonable, but she merely nodded towards the table, for him to sit down and have his breakfast. The atmosphere remained frosty, even frostier than usual, throughout the day. Towards the end of the afternoon he could stand it no longer. His impulse was to go back to the school, but he feared Gunter would still be there and had no wish to meet him. Instead he thought he'd go and see if Pete was at home, and maybe he could kip down on his floor.

He told his grandmother he had to leave because he had to work in the library the next morning to prepare for his lessons. She seemed to accept this, and they parted civilly, with the obligatory kisses and she even invited him to come back soon. He shouted *au revoir* to his grandfather down in his shed and got the same back.

Pete lived in a kind of bedsit in the servants' quarters in the apartment of a rather eccentric elderly man who seemed hardly to venture out of doors and wore a long embroidered dressing gown, cravat, and a Turkish cap. He looked like a villain from an old film. The building was in the 16th arrondissement, the poshest in Paris which had its own accent. There was no phone in the house so he'd just have to chance it and turn up. The landlord answered the door and looked somewhat taken aback when he asked if he could see Pete. Silently he ushered him in and pointed up the stairs toward to the top floor. Pete was in his room reading and listening to records. He said he was grateful for the excuse to go out. They went to the couple of bars they could find open at that hour on a Sunday evening. In no time, talk came around to Ingrid. Pete was firmly of the opinion that Steff should 'make a move,' as he put it.

'What about Gunter?' asked Steff.

'Gunter's in Germany.'

'Absence makes the heart grow fonder.'

'Out of sight, out of mind.'

Perhaps Pete was right. He was something of a Lothario and known for his success with the opposite sex, although he admitted he was going through a 'fallow patch' right then. In fact when Steff had called on him, he'd been listening to *Tous Les Garçons et Les Filles de Mon Age* – the huge hit for Françoise Hardy a couple of years back. She sang '*...all the boys and girls of my age walk along the street two by two...but I go alone...for I've no-one who loves me.*' Steff was no such Lothario. At university there'd been only a couple of short-lived flings. He did see though that his feelings for Ingrid were such that something had to give. It was just a question of whether he had the guts to do anything.

8

He bumped into Ingrid in the corridor of the assistants' rooms when he got back the next day. She greeted him warmly with a hug and a kiss.

'I'm cooking German sausages tonight. Would you like to come?'

'I'd love to. I'll bring wine,' he said, before thinking about what this might entail. Would Gunter be there? Too late to ask.

As it turned out, Gunter had left – for good.

'Things weren't going well for a while,' said Ingrid, as they sipped wine while the sausages sizzled in a pan on the hotplate. 'He came here so we could make a decision. He decided he wants his freedom – his freedom to go with someone else.'

'I'm sorry,' said Steff, not knowing what else to say.

'You needn't be,' she said. 'I'm not really. I knew there was no future.'

Steff's heart gave a leap, as if a huge weight had been lifted from his shoulders. But now wouldn't be a good time to 'make a move,' he reasoned, not on the rebound. He didn't have to. It just happened. The kissing and cuddling started before the knackwursts were ready. In fact the knackwursts had to wait while the kissing and cuddling came to their natural conclusion.

The next day, the world had changed. It was brighter and full of promise. The romance blossomed, and being young, they were not bothered by the narrowness of their beds – if anything, this seemed to add to the excitement. Without any formal or even informal announcement, they became recognised as a couple around the school. Mme Baxter drove them to see Van Gogh's grave at Auvers-sur-Oise – Ingrid had expressed an interest – and the café where he was staying when he shot himself. She took them back to dinner with her daughter Elodie and her boyfriend Ahmed. Steff had come to realise that Mme Baxter's notions of English life were sometimes dated. She served sea bass which they ate with fish knives she'd brought from London. She explained that these were the norm in English dining rooms (*comme ça* was the expression she used). Ahmed expressed disbelief. Mme Baxter appealed to Steff.

'They are, aren't they? Fish knives are *comme ça.*' As she said the *ça* she sliced the air with her hand and brought it down on the table, for emphasis – a characteristic gesture.

Steff had never seen a fish knife before, but he felt honour bound to agree.

The weirdest evening out they spent was when they were invited to dinner by another English teacher, Mme Jaurès, who was known to be rather odd and obsessed with signs of the zodiac. She had red hair and wore flowing kaftans. Mme Baxter had told Steff that at the end of a parent-teachers meeting the headmaster had asked if there were any more questions. Mme Jaurès stood up and asked him what sun sign he was.

She lived in a dilapidated cottage on the edge of the Sénart forest. She'd written directions in her imperfect English but they managed to find the cart track that led from the lane and then on to a path that twisted through the trees. They caught sight of the forbidding old house by the dim light that protruded through one of the windows. All the others seemed to be shuttered. As they walked towards it Ingrid said it reminded her of the witch's house in Hansel and Gretel.

'Maybe we should leave a trail of stones so we can find our way back,' she said. Steff laughed but could tell she was only half joking.

'It'll be really dark when we go home. Did we bring a torch?'

'No, *we* didn't,' said Steff.

Ingrid banged on the lacklustre brass knocker and they waited and waited some more. Ingrid hit it again, longer and harder and this time the door creaked open to reveal Mme Jaurès looking harassed. She was wearing a purple kaftan which was much too big for her. For a moment or two the three of them stood in silence and Steff wondered if she'd forgotten they were coming. He proffered the bottle of Chinon they'd brought which she grabbed unceremoniously.

'Oh good. Enter, enter,' she said in English.

The door opened out into a room cluttered with old furniture draped with various cloths and rugs. There were a couple of table lamps shrouded in diaphanous scarves and candles burning on the mantel shelf. The whole effect was somewhat lugubrious. In the middle of the room was a dining table where sat her two sons in their late teens, introduced as Bruno and Boris. They stood up and shook hands politely but exchanged looks which Steff interpreted as meaning they were there under protest and had their own ideas of how to make fun.

Mme Jaurès ushered them to the table and asked Steff to open the wine. She served a huge plate of snails in their shells. Steff quite liked them, cooked as they were with butter, parsley and garlic. Ingrid looked horrified but with a leg nudge from Steff started to pick at one gingerly and forked a little through gritted teeth. The sons looked on and smirked. This was followed by a whole ox tongue which, unlike his mother's, proved rather slimy as she sliced it. Ingrid looked as if she was about to throw up, pursing her lips and swallowing hard. It was accompanied by a dish of odd looking lumps which brought to mind dog dung.

'How do you say *topinambours* in English?' demanded their hostess.

'Jerusalem artichokes,' said Steff. He'd had them at his grandparents' and found them pretty distasteful.

'What a bizarre name,' she said and waded straight in to her favourite subject. 'What sun sign is your fazzer?' Steff wasn't completely sure but gave it his best shot.

'Virgo,' he said, and the sons sniggered. Their only contribution to the meal was throwing little pieces of bread at each other and making sounds like *zizi*, (willy), *ziz, zik, zak.*

'He must be revolting,' said their mother. Ingrid stifled a giggle, but Steff knew that she meant rebellious, and had translated from the French *revolté*.

'Not particularly,' said Steff, now perilously close to the giggles himself.

The feast continued with a salad of bitter chicory from the garden, a block of orange Maroilles cheese which stank like a farmyard, and plums which had been stewing on the windowsill, said Mme Jaurès with pride, for a year. All accompanied, once the Chinon was finished, by wine pressed by her father, presumably with his feet, which would have tasted too sour on chips. Ingrid had made a heroic effort but couldn't have had more than two or three mouthfuls of the entire repast, filling herself up with bread. Bruno and Boris maintained their *follie à deux* throughout, acknowledging the guests only with occasional smug sidelong glances and barely disguised titters. Steff had begun to think that they had planned the whole meal themselves.

By this time both Steff and Ingrid couldn't wait to get out of there, but there were more treats ahead. It transpired that their hostess was something of an artist. She insisted on showing them her 'arts' (for one dreadful moment Steff thought she'd said arse) and shooed them into what must have been her bedroom. It was lined with amateurish daubs. The eye was immediately drawn to two large canvasses propped against the wall, one of Bruno, the other of Boris, both of them sitting on the toilet. The subjects slouched in the doorway eyeing the guests with amused disdain, as if daring them to disapprove. Steff glanced at Ingrid who, like him, was taking deep breaths. Mme Jaurès looked from one to the other expectantly.

'They're...original,' managed Steff.

'Sank you,' said Mme Jaurès, pleased.

'Thank *you*. For an...unforgettable evening. And now, we really must be going.'

Ingrid fairly wrung her hands in gratitude. 'Uh, do you have a torch we could borrow? We forgot to bring one.'

'Of course,' and she shuffled past her lounging sons. Steff half expected her to come back with a hurricane lamp, but she produced a surprisingly modern one. After more pleasantries were exchanged (the sons had disappeared) they took their leave. Barely out of earshot, they laughed so hard they had to hold each other up. Back in Steff's room, Ingrid gorged herself on bread and Boursin and they shared a bottle of acceptable plonk.

In those first weeks of rapturous young love, Steff gave barely a thought to his quest to discover what happened to his aunt. As the Easter vacation approached, though, he began to cotton on to the fact that his time in Paris would before long be coming to an end. Ingrid had asked him to come to Berlin for the holidays which he'd jumped at. So if he was to get anywhere with his search, he'd have to get a move on. He pondered his next step. He'd always remembered passing the school where his aunt had taught when his mother brought him to the French capital all those years ago, and how mysteriously dismissive she'd been about making further enquiries.

By this time he'd become quite friendly with the formidable woman who ran the *Documentation* centre.

He went to see her and explained what he was after. Did schools hold records of teachers in the past?'

'Normally, yes.' She seemed intrigued with his pursuit. 'As you probably know the Nazis invaded Paris very quickly so although there was a lot of hardship and confusion for the people, there was little destruction like there was in London.'

Buoyed by this, he rang up the Lycée Émile Zola and managed to get through to the deputy headmistress.

Yes, she said, they should have those records. He could come in and see M Hulot in the *Documentation* who acted as their de facto archivist. She'd make an appointment. Steff was delightfully surprised at how simple this turned out to be after months, indeed years, of hesitation.

M Hulot was a tall, gangly man in his fifties who sported a goatee and a purple bow tie with white dots, of the kind only otherwise seen on professors in American movies. He too was eager to help. Steff often heard it said, by Brits and indeed the rural French, that Parisians were rude, but he'd never found them so. Direct, yes. They would talk to you in the shops, as they did back in Aberystwyth: old ladies, mainly. When he first went to London he used to do the same but people would look at him as if he were mad. When he went back to Aber in the holidays he would not say anything when he went into a shop and was considered offish. The French were more polite and formal than the British as well. He and Ingrid had visited the museum in Compiègne, where both the 1918 and 1940 armistices were signed in a railway carriage in a wood. The second, of course, was when the French surrendered and Hitler came in person to sign it, relishing no doubt his revenge for the humiliation of the first. Steff still held a certain fascination for anything to do with rail and so it had an added attraction for him. There was a booklet of etiquette issued to British squaddies in the First World War. It urged them to use *Madame* and *Monsieur* when calling to strangers instead of 'Oi!' To this day he would be addressed as *Monsieur* by people, including children, he didn't know.

M Hulot went over to a large wooden cabinet with a roll-down shutter which he rolled up to reveal ranks of arch lever files.

'Céleste Dujardin, you say? And you think she taught here during the war?'

He ran his fingers along the files and stopped at one half way along.

'Ah yes. Here we are.'

He pulled it out and brought it over to his desk where Steff was sitting.

'Now let's see.'

He thumbed through the pages methodically. Steff waited anxiously.

'Ah yes. Here we are,' said M Hulot again, and took quite some time reading what was before him.

'Your aunt did indeed teach here.'

'Until when?'

He consulted the file again.

'1946.'

'So she taught here throughout the war?' said Steff. She hadn't left the city like a million other citizens. M Hulot nodded. Steff's mouth was dry with nervous anticipation.

'Do you know what happened to her afterwards?'

'No. We wouldn't have those records.'

'What about an address?'

'Yes, we have that.'

He gave an address in rue Oberkampf.

'Is that nearby?'

'Indeed. Just down the road. You turn left at the front entrance, go down avenue de la République, and turn left at the traffic lights and there you are.'

He was halfway down the street when he realised with a jolt that it was within the realm of possibility that in a few minutes he could come face to face with the aunt that no-one in his family had heard from for years. He quickened his step, and again wondered why neither his mother or grandparents had come this far in trying to find her, considering how easy it had turned out to be.

He found the apartment building halfway up the street. It was typically Parisian, of cream-coloured stone with wrought-iron Juliette balconies on the windows of the lower floors and huge wooden double doors on the entrance. He looked up to the top, where the windows were smaller and without balconies. The address gave no clue as to which floor his aunt would have occupied. There was a brass bell on the right hand side which he pressed, and waited. There was no answer. He rang again. Presently the door opened and a small woman emerged dragging a shopping trolley. Steff caught the door as it closed and murmured thanks to the shopper.

On the left hand side were rows of letter boxes and to the right a couple of steps up to a small room or office which Steff took to be the concierge's lair. Through the glass-panelled door he saw a roll top desk, a comfy chair and a table with a gas ring, kettle and coffee things. A radio was playing popular music. No-one was inside. Without knowing why he rapped on the glass just in case. But the door stayed closed. He turned around to inspect the letter boxes. Each had a printed name plate in a brass frame, except for two or three which had handwritten names stuck over the originals. He began reading them from top to bottom, left to right, hoping against hope that he'd find Mlle Dujardin. This was supposing a great deal, that she still lived there after all these years and that she'd never married. He came to the one on the bottom right without any luck. He read them again, and again, but her name didn't miraculously appear.

An elderly man wearing a trilby approached from the courtyard at the end of the hall.

'Excuse me, monsieur, I'm trying to find my aunt, Céleste Dujardin, who used to live here, or maybe still does. Do you happen to know her?'

Was it Steff's imagination or did the man look slightly uneasy, shifty even?

'I'm sorry. I don't know anyone of that name.'

Steff cursed the fact that he had no picture of his aunt, and had never seen one. He couldn't even give a description.

'Could I ask you, how long have you lived here?'

Now the man looked distinctly nervous.

'Could I ask you why you're asking?'

'Well, as I said, I'm looking for my aunt. I know she was living here until at least 1946.'

'That's a long time ago. I wasn't here then. And now, if you'll excuse me, monsieur, I have an appointment to keep.'

'One last question, if I may, do you know where the concierge is?' Steff stretched out his right arm as if to stop him leaving.

'Probably gossiping with one or other of the occupants as usual. I didn't see her in the courtyard.'

'And how long has she been here?'

'She was here when I came here. Now, good day.' He tipped his hat and exited, rather hurriedly.

The concierge then might be the key to his aunt's whereabouts. If she'd moved she must have left a forwarding address. He glanced again at her door, and fumbled around in his pocket for the little book and pencil he'd brought to make notes. He tore out a page and leant it against one of the letter boxes. He wrote who he was and who he was looking for, gave the school's address, asking her to contact him, folding it over, putting a stamp inside and sliding it under the concierge's door.

That evening he told Ingrid about his investigations. She was enthusiastic about his chances of success. For the next few days as soon he was awake he walked down to the lodge at the school gates. Here were the staff's pigeon holes for mail. There was a letter from his mother giving the news from home. A couple of days later a postcard from Pete suggesting they meet up at the weekend. Nothing from the concierge. He waited a week and then he could stand the suspense no longer, and when no letter came he went up to the apartment building in rue Oberkampf.

This time when he rang the bell the door was opened promptly to reveal a buxom woman wearing a housecoat and a scarf around her hair. Must be in her sixties, Steff judged, so there was a good chance she would have been here during the war. He introduced himself.

'Ah yes, Monsieur Lewis (she pronounced it leveess). I'm so sorry – I've been meaning to write but I haven't found the time. I'm on my feet morning til night, you know.'

She invited him into her sanctum, ushered him into the armchair and set about making him a cup of coffee. She introduced herself as Mme Jacquin.

'The thing is, I can't remember anyone of that name. I came here just before the end of the war so from the date you mentioned in your note I think I would have known if she lived here.'

'Her name was Céleste. You don't remember anyone of that name?'

'No...no, I can't say I do. Generally I know the residents by their surname, unless I become particularly friendly with them.'

'The lycée where she taught told me this was her address until 1946 at least. You can't think of a single woman, round about thirty years of age living here at that time?'

'No...no I can't call to mind any single women then. Couples, families, some single men and women but they were a lot older.'

She seemed sincere in her efforts to help him, and intrigued by such a challenge.

'Might she be married by that time?'

'Well, yes it's entirely possible but I have no way of knowing. She'd become estranged from my family, you see.'

'Ah, and why was that, if you don't mind me asking?'

'We don't know. It's a mystery and I'm trying to solve it.'

'You have my sympathies. Of course, during the war many people left and some lost contact with their loved ones.'

'But that's not the case here. She was known to have lived here until after the war.'

'Yes, I see. A mystery, as you say.'

'If she had married, can you tell me the names of young couples at the time?'

'It's such a long time ago. There were a few married couples here, some with small babies, but I'm afraid I can't remember all their names. There are more than eighty apartments here.'

'And you don't think some of the older residents might be able to help?'

'Well, without a picture or description…'

'I know. If only…'

He thought that long ago he asked his mother if she had one and she didn't. But he couldn't be sure. Or maybe his grandparents would have one. That was his only hope, but judging by their past reactions when he'd mentioned his aunt, it wouldn't be an easy or pleasant task to ask them for one. He said as much to Mme Jacquin.

'Well, you do that. Meanwhile I'll rack my brains to

see if anything comes to light. And maybe ask around here a bit. I've got your address and if something turns up I'll write to you this time. I promise,' she said with a sympathetic smile and a rather saucy glint in her eye.

Steff was crestfallen. So near and yet so far. A picture of his aunt was the only tack he could think of. He wandered into the courtyard, a pleasant space of cobbled paths between beds full of plants in pots. It was surrounded on all sides by more flats, without balconies. He surveyed them all, thinking that his aunt might be behind one of them at that very minute. But Mme Jacquin was right – he could hardly knock on every single door in the hope of finding her. Or could he?

It was only when he was on the metro back to the Gare de Lyon that he suddenly had a flash. Of course, he *had* seen a picture of his aunt – the one he found in the attic years back. That was how this whole thing started. In his mind's eye he saw quite an angelic little girl with curly fair hair, but who looked sad. Would that be of any help? She would have changed so much in those intervening years. He had no idea of what had happened to the photo. Maybe it was still behind the trunk in the attic where he'd left it. Could his mother have taken it? Would she still have it now? And would his grandparents have one of her as a grown woman? He very much doubted it. And even if they had, they probably wouldn't give him it. It was as if they'd brushed her out of their life entirely and eternally.

He'd been wondering how much, if anything, to tell his grandparents and mother of his discoveries. Now he'd have to.

9

Ingrid's classes finished before his at Easter and for some reason she wanted to return to Berlin straightaway. He decided to stay on and get the night train from the Gare du Nord. It left just before midnight and would arrive the next morning. He was surprised when he got there at how old the train was, especially the *wagon lit*, panelled in wood with plush furnishings. He walked further than his carriage to check if there was a steam locomotive at the front but it was a relatively modern engine. His thoughts turned to what his lecturer Anne had told him about the Jewish deportations from Paris in the early 1940s and it gave him a feeling of unease making the journey, imagining the horror of those who made it just a couple of decades before.

The compartment was a two-berth but as the train pulled out no-one else appeared. He'd bought a bottle of wine and after a few healthy swigs fell easily asleep. He was wakened in the early hours by three East German guards, unsmiling and taciturn. Bleary-eyed, he fumbled for his passport from his rucksack and handed it over to the nearest one, a young fair-haired man who inspected it carefully, and asked him in English why he was going to Berlin.

'To see my girlfriend,' said Steff. As far as he was aware, this was the first time he'd used the word and it felt good. 'For a couple of weeks.'

'You are English and you live in Paris?'

Steff let the 'English' pass.

'Yes, I'm teaching there for a year. I go back to London in the summer.'

This seemed to satisfy the guard and he handed it back with an officious flick of his wrist.

Steff went back to sleep and woke again when light started slipping through a gap at the bottom of the window blind. He let it up and surveyed the countryside. It was the first time he'd been in Germany and he had that pleasant sensation of seeing even everyday little things with wonder. What he saw took him by surprise. He'd thought of East Germany as a strong power, with the sporting prowess and military might that was presented to the outside world. What he saw was a throwback to another age: dirt tracks leading to decrepit little villages; farmsteads with chickens and geese in earthen runs enclosed with rough and ready fences made of branches and twigs. In one of them a bent little old lady wearing a drab headscarf and long skirt was scattering feed to the hens. It could have been a scene from decades before. There wasn't much traffic on the roads, only a few of those Trabant things chugging along.

It could not have been a greater contrast as they crossed into West Berlin. There were old buildings of course, many of them still bearing the scars of war, and even piles of rubble on lots here and there. Gleaming glass towers were going up too, as if to obliterate the past. But Steff couldn't help imagining what the pre-war houses had been witness to – this, and this, and this.

Ingrid was on the station platform to meet him as the train pulled in. It was a wonderfully romantic if somewhat clichéd reunion, even though they had been apart only for a few days. Steff shrugged off the past and tried to embrace the present. But as they took the U-bahn to Kreuzberg where she lived his thoughts rewound: the yellow trains were old and rickety with high-backed wooden seats. History was everywhere in this city. He was consumed with curiosity about what Ingrid and her contemporaries made of all that had happened twenty years or so ago. They would have been born after the war, of course, so would have no personal memories but their parents and grandparents would. He thought it indelicate to ask. He would have to think of a way.

Kreuzberg though was very much of the present and recognisably a student quarter: somewhat scruffy with posters for pop concerts and such, full of coffee bars, record stores and boutiques with the latest young fashions which could have been straight out of swinging London. Ingrid lived with two fellow students, Dieter and Birgit, on the second floor of an old house which looked characteristically German to Steff's mind. They were friendly in their greetings in a casual, student kind of way. And easy going. They drank beer and listened to American and British pop music. Hippyish, Steff thought with approval. Or maybe bohemian would be a better word.

Over the next few days Ingrid gave him a tour of West Berlin: the Kaiser Wilhelm church with its stump of the old nave and the huge new hexagonal belfry of stained glass; the ruins of the Reichstag; the walled-up Brandenburg gate. The centre of the old city, the Mitte, was the other side of the wall in the East, Ingrid told him. Steff made continued efforts to enjoy the present and look to the future, but for him a sinister pall hung over the city, and even on the Kufürstendamm with its luxury shops he could almost hear the clatter of marching jackboots.

It was she who brought up the past.

'You must be thinking what we young people make of the Nazi era?' she said.

'Well, yes, but...but I didn't like to ask.'

'I understand. It's not easy. Of course we weren't born then so in one way it seems like ancient history. But in another way all our families were affected.'

Her father had been conscripted into the army when he was eighteen, sent to the Russian front, and taken prisoner of war where he stayed for three years. He was never quite the same again and died quite young. His father had been a university lecturer in humanities and the family were staunchly opposed to Hitler's regime, but didn't have much choice. Two of her uncles, one on her father's side and one on her mother's, were killed on the Western front. She didn't say it, and certainly didn't try to gloss over the Nazi years, but Steff could see that many ordinary Germans had been victims too. It showed how people could be manipulated by tyrannical power. Indeed it was by no means easy for Ingrid's generation. What a burden on young shoulders.

On the Saturday after a breakfast of bread rolls, hard-boiled eggs and coffee, Ingrid said she had a surprise for him.

'We're going to the East,' she said.

'We can do that?' He'd been wondering if it was possible.

'Well, it should be easy for you with your British passport. I should be able to get a day visa to visit relatives but they can refuse and don't give a reason.'

The plan was to take her aunt Hildy and cousin Jurgen to one of the top hotels on Unter den Linden for lunch. Only pensioners were allowed to visit the West – and top-ranking party members, no doubt. They got the U-bahn to Friedrichstrasse Station where the crossing point was. First they queued up for the Western border control which was straightforward. Then they had to push through reinforced doors to a narrow passage lined with laminate wood. East German guards stood behind high glass booths. Steff found it claustrophobic and oppressive, even though he got through without a hitch. Ingrid on the other hand was asked many questions and for a few nerve-racking minutes it seemed there was a problem. Eventually the guard, rather reluctantly it seemed, stamped her passport with a thump. They emerged into a modern circular hall with huge glass windows where long queues of drab, sad-looking East Germans were waiting to cross. Ingrid told him the building was known locally as the *Tränenpalast* – the Palace of Tears – where families were separated.

'And what do you make of this whole East business?' Steff asked Ingrid, emboldened by her openness.

She sighed.

'It's so complicated. The DDR state was born out of the ruins of war. They wanted to promise future generations it would never happen again – that they would build a new Germany for the common good. In fact that's what their national anthem is called: *Auferstanden aus Ruinen* – Risen from Ruins. I quite like it.'

She started humming it softly.

'In a way I suppose I see it as a noble experiment to build a new future for all people. But you can see what it's turning into. People are killed for trying to escape. They dig tunnels, hide children in suitcases, and one tried to jump over the wall with a pole like they do in the Olympics. Neighbour informs on neighbour if they think they're subversive.'

That summed it up neatly, thought Steff. They strolled towards Unter den Linden and it felt like a totally different city, a city that time forgot. The citizens looked colourless and downtrodden, and there was nothing like the glitzy shops of the West. A couple of youths were wearing their hair longer than other males (but only just) and rather cheap looking jeans which looked oddly homemade. Traffic was sparse and consisted entirely of those two-stroke Trabants, almost all of them a dull cream colour. Old yellow trams rattled down the street. There was something else that made the place so distinctive, but Steff couldn't put his finger on it.

They had a bit of time before lunch and Ingrid showed him the sights of Unter den Linden, a wide thoroughfare of grand but shabby buildings of pale yellow stone. It would have been the Champs Elysés of the day. Some of the facades still bore bullet and shrapnel holes.

They walked down past a hotel which Ingrid said was the first headquarters of the Nazi Party, the Opera House, History Museum, and on to Museuminsel – Museum Island – in the middle the River Spree. More grandiose edifices of yore, and the huge blackened cathedral. Beyond that was the gigantic TV tower which was still being built, like a spear soaring into the sky. It was clearly visible throughout the Western city – presumably a statement of how advanced the German Democratic Republic was.

On the way back up Ingrid showed him Bebelplatz, the huge square in front of the library and university where in 1933 students made a bonfire of books – Jewish, Marxist, Socialist or anything the Nazis didn't approve of.

'Are there any kind of memorials or whatever to the Jews who were exterminated?' asked Steff.

'No, I don't think so.' Ingrid's voice held a note of apology. 'Maybe it's too soon for them. People want to forget before they remember. Maybe one day…'

Lunch was in the gleaming glass and concrete Brandenburger Hotel, virtually the only new building on the street.

'We'll have to be careful what we say,' said Ingrid. 'It's where foreign diplomats and such stay. The Stasi know everything that goes on here.'

The restaurant was a large hall with lace curtains covering its vast windows There were rows of round tables, most of them empty, with uncomfortable looking wooden chairs. Ingrid scanned the room, gave a small wave and made her way to the middle, where sat a woman and a boy who must have been in his late teens.

Ingrid introduced them as her aunt and cousin. Hildy was younger than expected – he only now realised that he'd subconsciously formed a picture of her. In her late thirties, he judged, wearing a pale green woollen coat with large buttons, a sort of imitation of Western fashions. The youth was in sombre clothes – a brown kind of windcheater – and had cropped fair hair. They stood up and hugged Ingrid, with both joy and sorrow it seemed, and formally shook Steff's hand.

They took their places and Steff noticed there was a tub of lard on the white paper tablecloth, alongside a small vase of plastic cornflowers.

Conversation was strained. The relatives spoke no English and his schoolboy German was not up to much, although he'd picked a few things up with Ingrid and even with his few days in the city. There was a limited choice on the menu, and they all ordered pork chops, boiled potatoes and pickled cucumbers, with apple strudel to follow. There was beer to drink.

The three caught up on family news. Jurgen didn't say much, but seemed to find Steff with his longish hair, Western jeans and leather jacket intriguing. In due course Steff was able to join in, albeit in a desultory way. He wanted to find out about their life and home, but was aware of the warning Ingrid had given him. He settled for asking where they lived. He understood that Hildy said they lived in a flat in Kopenhagner Strasse in a district called Prenzlauer Berg.

'It's in a typical Berlin apartment block called an Altbauhaus,' said Ingrid 'It's a house of four or five floors built around the beginning of the century. The wall is at the end of their street.'

Hildy looked round her nervously, leant forward into the table and lowered her voice. Steff caught some of what she was saying: 'old lady…flat upstairs…wall…Sunday morning…family.'

In hushed tones, Ingrid filled in the gaps for him.

'There's an old lady – how would you say, an invalid – in the flat upstairs and her whole family lives on the other side of the wall. She remembers it being built and wasn't allowed to leave the building. Every Sunday morning at 11 o'clock her neighbour on the top floor helps her up to her flat where she can see over the wall. Her son, daughter and their children and grandchildren stand on the other side and wave and go like this…'

She blew kisses.

'Es ist traurig,' Steff managed.

'Ja, ist traurig,' said Hildy, and she looked the saddest woman Steff had ever met. Jurgen remained impassive, looking around him in an evasive manner. Conversation after this became even more restrained. Ingrid, usually so eloquent, looked ill at ease and seemed not to know what to say, what words of comfort she could offer. When it came time to go, there were tearful hugs for Ingrid and warm handshakes for Steff. It had clearly been a rare treat for them. Ingrid had insisted on paying the bill, and explained on the way back to Kreuzberg that they wouldn't have been able to afford it. She asked him for his impressions of the East. He didn't find it easy to put into words.

'It's, well, like nothing I've ever witnessed before. It's like stepping back in time. I can see that maybe the GDR's intentions were noble to begin with, rebuilding a peaceful and caring nation, making sure everyone had a decent life.'

It came to him suddenly what was so different, what had been missing: an absence of advertising, billboards, neon lights, commercialism. He said as much.

'I know,' said Ingrid. 'Sometimes I think it's...,' she searched for the word, 'refreshing.'

'Yeah,' said Steff. 'But it seems too high a price to pay: the price of personal freedom. Surely it's wrong, this separation, division, this surveillance.'

Ingrid nodded slowly.

In fact he'd found the whole Berlin experience absorbing, exhilarating even. He rather thought it had given him the travel bug.

10

Back in Paris, Steff knew that it was time to grasp the nettle and tell his mother and grandmother (he'd surely get no joy from his grandfather) about what he'd been up to, and to try to get a photograph of his aunt. He mulled over his approach long and hard, and decided he would talk to his mother first. Ingrid encouraged him – it was something he had to do. He considered various approaches as to how to tackle his mother. Face to face would be best, he figured, but that would mean a long and costly journey back to Aberystwyth for a short visit – he didn't want to miss any classes. So it would be have to be mouth to ear, but a public phone box would simply hoover up coins.

In the end it was Mme Baxter who came up with a solution. He'd asked her if there was a phone in the school he could use for an important call home, for which he'd pay, of course.

'I've got a better idea. You can make a call from my house, and ask your mother to call you back straightaway,' she said. 'You can come for dinner.'

He and Ingrid went, gladly and gratefully. Mme

Baxter had made boeuf bourguignon with tiny onions and lardons. It was a deep, dark purple colour and was the tastiest casserole either of them had ever had. Mme Baxter looked pleased at their compliments but made a show of shrugging them off: it was nothing, really.

The phone was on a desk in a little room she used as a study, so he had complete privacy. He and his mother exchanged snippets of news and assured each other that all was well. He could tell though, that his mother suspected there was a reason for the call, but she didn't ask him directly.

'And I've got something else to tell you. I've found out where the aunt lived.'

'Oh Steff, are you still harking on about that?'

'Well, it's a mystery that keeps niggling at me. I just want to see if I can find out what happened to her.'

'I've tried to tell you, she cut herself off from the family years ago. We made every effort to track her down for ages, after the war even, all to no avail. It became clear that she wanted nothing to do with us.'

'But aren't you at all curious? About why she should be that way?'

'Not anymore, no. She hurt us. Anyway, this call is costing money so we can't just keep on talking.'

Steff gave a brief summary of how the school had given him the address, but the concierge didn't know anyone of that surname. He was just about to ask his mother whether she knew if Céleste married, but of course she couldn't know and the question would annoy her.

'The thing is, if I had a photo of her, I could show it to the concierge. Do you have one you could send?'

'No, I do not.'

'What about that one I found in the attic?'

'Oh, God knows what happened to that. It was years ago.' His mother was getting quietly ruffled now, he could tell. He'd have one last quick stab.

'Would Mamie have one?'

'I really don't know. I doubt it. Oh, don't go pestering her, Steff. It would bring back painful memories.'

Back in his room, he told Ingrid about the call.

'How can I go against my mother's wishes?' he asked.

'I would think that just to ask for a photograph wouldn't be pestering, as you say. You needn't say anything about the school or the flat. It's important to you, isn't it?'

'Yes, I suppose it is. I couldn't say why. Just part of my past. But also…' he trailed off, not quite knowing what he wanted to say.

'Also…what?'

'It's kind of hard to put into words. It's as if…it's as if, well, they're covering something up. As if there's something they don't want me to know.'

'But surely that would have nothing to do with you. No painful memories, I mean.'

'No.'

Ingrid was right. He would not pester his grandmother, just ask a casual question about a photograph.

He determined to go to Conflans the next weekend. His time in Paris was quickly coming to an end and he knew it was now or never. For him and Ingrid it was a confusing time, both looking forward to going back to friends and families but having to cope with separation, however temporary, and an unknowable future for them. The sense of an ending was underlined one evening when Mme Moulec came knocking on his door, wearing her habitual blue overall and a worried expression.

'Monsieur Moulec is not well,' she said, waving her hands close to her forehead in confusion. 'I don't know what's wrong with him.'

As he followed her back to their rooms, she explained with halting breaths that they were retiring, and had been to a little presentation in the headmaster's house. He found her husband stretched out on his bed, red-faced and sobbing quietly. He was mumbling a little incoherently, '…finished…all over…'

'Did he have something to drink at the presentation?'

'Oh yes,' said his wife. 'They gave us champagne. Well, him anyway. I don't drink, and neither does he normally.'

'I think he might have had a bit too much,' said Steff as gently as he could. 'Why don't you make him some coffee and I'll have a little talk with him.'

Steff managed to get him to sit up and gave him such words of comfort that he could think of, new beginnings, opportunities and so on. The old man had at least stopped weeping. It was clear that he hated the thought of retirement. Steff looked around, and was surprised to find that their accommodation was merely three rooms like his with connecting doors. They must have lived here most of their working lives, thought Steff. Single beds.

No wonder M Moulec was fearful of the future, of the unknown, imagining the worst.

Mme Moulec came back with the coffee and after a while her husband calmed down and sobered up. He said they'd been dreaming of this day for ages – they'd saved up to put a deposit on a little cottage back in Brittany – but now it had come, it was a bit of a shock. His wife was calmer too and offered her own support: it would take a while for both of them to get used to it but just think what a fine time they'd have in the cottage by the sea. He left them consoling each other, if not entirely convincing each other. It must be awful to grow old, he thought.

Next day he wrote a postcard to his grandparents informing them of his plans. He knew that they would be waiting on his visit, however distant they were when he was there, as they rarely left the house these days. He sent one to Rita and Bob too, and they invited him to lunch on the Sunday, which at least was something to look forward to. He'd go up on Saturday afternoon and return on Monday morning: the lunch would no doubt be a rather prolonged affair if he knew anything about them. He badly wanted Ingrid to go with him, but she had a friend visiting from Berlin. Thinking it over, maybe it would be best if he were there alone.

His grandmother and even his grandfather were evidently pleased to see him, in their own way, and his grandmother embraced him warmly. But they were getting older and frailer, and even more turned in on themselves, so their joy soon waned. They seemed obsessed with their routines, and his Papie retired to his shed while Mamie busied herself with mysterious kitchen rituals. Steff went up to his bedroom, claiming he had studying to do, and read for a while, at the same time pondering the best way and time to broach the photo question. Monday morning, he decided: if she did react badly, it wouldn't tarnish the weekend.

His grandmother had got used to his visits next door and while she was clearly not enthusiastic about them, didn't make a fuss either. He found Rita and Bob on the terrace with their guests sipping drinks and snacking on Rita's customary array of nibbles. Sophie and Bernard were there, along with a lively, charismatic Irish woman called Anna who taught with Rita. She told stories about her colourful life, including her sacking from a convent school south of Dublin where she taught briefly. While taking her class to the little village she'd nipped into the Post Office for a pint of Guinness (there were pumps in many a little shop in Ireland, apparently).

Sophie asked Steff if he'd found out anything about the aunt, and he filled her in.

'You don't happen to have a photo of her do you?
'Afraid not.'

'And you don't know if she was married?'

'No. In fact now you mention it, I never heard of any man in her life when we got older. It struck me as unusual because we young women were always talking about men, or boys I suppose they were then.'

She gave a self-deprecating laugh and rolled her eyes as if to say what silly little things they were. Bernard looked at her with disapproval.

As they went inside for the main course of cassoulet, conversation turned to music. Jacques Brel was playing in the background and Steff along with the others greatly admired his lyricism and passionate performances. Since Bob had introduced him to the classic musicians of the day last time, Steff had listened to as much as he could and now felt more comfortable joining in their conversations about them. Bob put on Georges Moustaki then Juliette Gréco, keen perhaps to show off the cream of French chanson, and seemed impressed at Steff's comments, jerking his head downwards and raising his eyebrows is if to say 'the kid knows something.' And Steff did appreciate the poetry of their songs. Anna seemed to take the cue for her own number, and stood up singing *Dirty Old Town* with swaying hips and swirling arms:

> *I met my love by the gas works wall*
> *Dreamed a dream by the old canal*
> *I kissed my girl by the factory wall*
> *Dirty old town*
> *Dirty old town*

Quite a performance, thought Steff, and what a contrast to the atmosphere next door. Somehow talk then moved on to politics. None of them proved to be a fan of President de Gaulle. It came as something of a surprise to Steff – he'd imagined he'd be something of a national hero after leading the Free French from London during the war. Steff had a fondness for the French House in Soho with its wood panelling and black and white photographs adorning the walls. It was said that de Gaulle met there with his government in exile, and was a haunt of writers and artists like Dylan Thomas and Francis Bacon. It still drew a bohemian and eccentric crowd. Steff had walked in there one evening and standing at the bar there was a colourfully dressed woman with an equally colourful parrot on her shoulder. He related all this but his audience were unimpressed. They spoke of de Gaulle's handling of the Algerian crisis, and the aftermath of independence which sowed turmoil in France. Bob said students were restless and there was talk of revolution.

The others left about four. Steff thought he should go too: he was feeling decidedly sloshed. There was a ring at the door, and Bob went to answer it, thinking someone had forgotten something. But it was two Jehovah's Witnesses. Instead of slamming the door in their face as some might have done, Bob invited them in for a chat. He brought out a bottle of cognac, which they refused. He poured himself and Steff a slug. He lit up a Gauloise and seemed purposely to blow it in their faces as they sat opposite at the dining room table. He's going to enjoy winding them up, thought Steff, and he was up for the spectacle. Bob started fairly gently, asking them how they could prove that God exists. They quoted the Bible and asked in turn if there was no God and heaven, what was the point of life on earth.

'Good question,' said Bob. 'That's what we all have to figure out for ourselves.'

'But wouldn't you like to think there's an afterlife, where we're rewarded for leading good lives on earth?' asked the younger of the two men.

'Good God, no,' said Bob. 'The only way to get through it all is the thought that one day it'll end.'

The men looked startled, and even more so when Bob declared himself a Communist, which Steff knew not to be true from conversations he'd had with him. At this point they stood up, said polite goodbyes, and left.

Steff woke with quite a hangover the next morning. He'd stumbled in as quietly as he could the evening before and shouted from the entrance hall that he had a headache and was going up to bed. There was hot chocolate and croissants awaiting him on the kitchen table when he emerged, and a rather crusty grandmother. She thawed slightly over breakfast when he told her he had to leave soon because he had classes that afternoon. It was a lie, but he didn't want to prolong the agony. As he got up from the table and picked up his bag, he said, 'Oh and by the way, you don't happen to have a photo of Céleste do you, as a young woman?'

'Why?' was all his grandmother said, holding her cup just before it reached her lips.

'Just curious that's all. If you see it from my point of view, I've got a mysterious aunt I've never met.' He added as some sort of palliative, 'And never likely to.'

'Stéphane, I've asked you to forget all about her. She turned her back on us.'

She finally took a sip of chocolate.

'And no, I don't have a photograph. She might have had some but must have taken them with her when she left. Never to get in touch again.'

Steff tried to picture that moment, when she closed

the front door and made her way to her little flat, as he saw it, in rue Oberkampf. Why did she never come back? Why? The question haunted him. As he opened that very same door, he looked back into the kitchen and thought he saw his grandmother wipe a tear from her eye.

11

Steff's graduation ceremony was held at the Albert Hall, and his degree was given by the Queen Mother, the Chancellor of London University. His parents got the train up from Aberystwyth. They were no enthusiastic royalists, his mother being of an *egalité, fraternité* disposition and his father tending to the view that the English monarchy had been an occupying force, but when he stepped up on the platform to receive his degree he looked up to where they were sitting and he could see them beaming with pride. The Queen Mother was one of those people who bestowed a smile as if you were her favourite person in the room – although Steff inclined to his parents' views of the monarchy.

He got a job as a copywriter on a travel magazine called Voyages. His languages were a bonus as it was an Anglo-French venture. He'd picked up quite a bit of German with Ingrid, and because of his fluent French found it relatively easy to get by in Italian and Spanish with a little study and practice. His Latin A Level helped. There wasn't much call for Welsh in the international travel market.

Ingrid had come over to London for a couple of weeks in the summer after their year in Paris. He'd moved into a dilapidated old house in Hackney with five other students ready for his final year. It was a bit of a dump, truth be told, but Ingrid seemed to find the place full of charm. She'd been to London before on a school trip, so somewhat to Steff's surprise was not interested in the usual sights. Instead she wanted to explore the East End – she'd read about the misery and mayhem during the war. He had to mug up on it himself, and found it an eye-opener.

Steff found a walking tour called East Enders in the War. It started at St Paul's and the guide was a lively young woman who was brought up in Bow. She said a lot of information she was giving was first hand from people who'd lived through it. Steff particularly liked one story of a couple during an air raid. The man had left their house when the siren started up, but saw his wife was not following him. He shouted to her through the upstairs window.

'Come'n Ethel – we've got to go to the shelter.'

'I can't find me teeth,' said Ethel.

'They're dropping bombs, not bleedin' sandwiches,' said her exasperated husband.

Ingrid loved that too. Her visit was a success and at that time they both still foresaw a long term future together. Steff was due to go over to Hamburg the following summer, but somehow it didn't happen. The relationship trickled away, beyond his grasp, and it felt like gold dust slipping through his fingers. He thought back to their last parting at the airport gates at Gatwick. Had there been a sense then, an inkling, that there was no future? He didn't think so. In a way that was the hardest part – there was no formal break up, no goodbyes, no acrimony, and for quite a while afterwards they wrote to each other now and then. He wondered if Ingrid also sensed this gloaming, and if she was as sad as he was. Neither of them had the courage to broach the subject in their letters. So he was left with an agonising mix of regret and hope.

On the magazine Steff progressed to writing his own pieces and after a couple of years went freelance to write for other magazines. One of his first features was about a trip he made on the Trans-Siberian Express from Moscow to Beijing. It was his own idea, of course, given his long-lasting fascination with all things rail. His editor, a rambunctious portly little man given to wearing braces, was not keen.

'Who the hell wants to spend a week on a train in Siberia?' he yelled.

'Well I do, for a start. And that's the whole point. Give them a window on the world beyond Benidorm. Something they can only experience by reading about it.'

With a lot of persistence, and maybe a little pestering, Steff ground him down. The trip turned out to be quite an adventure. It didn't get off to a flying start – literally. There was a delay at Heathrow because, said the British Airways captain, they weren't happy with the quality of the water to make the tea. How British, though Steff. How reassuring.

About an hour after takeoff there was a loud bang and some sparks on the wing opposite his seat. There were a couple of screams. It took a few seconds before the same reassuring voice came over the tannoy.

'Uh, some of you might have noticed that – there's nothing to worry about at all – a flap has blown off the the right-side wing. Now, as a precaution, we're turning back to Heathrow and we'll make every effort to get you on the next flight to Moscow.

The plane started its descent. The guy next to Steff looked at him quizzically and asked, 'Moscow?'

'No, back to London,' said Steff.

His neighbour looked perplexed, as well he might. He clearly didn't have much English. All Steff could do was make an upward motion with his outstretched hand, turn around, and come back down again. Now the man was positively alarmed.

They did get on another flight to Moscow a couple of hours later. Steff's train left Yaroslavsky station at midnight, and there were only two a week. It would be touch and go. The inevitable hold-ups at Immigration, the long taxi queues, and the mad dash through the city meant that he'd all but given up on hope of making it. He was on the platform with two minutes to spare, and as he jumped up through the nearest door, the whistle blew. As the train lurched into jerky life, he wobbled his way along the corridor until he found his four-berth sleeper. He opened and closed the door as quietly as he could, and was relieved to be greeted with the sound of gentle and uninterrupted snoring. He climbed onto one of the top bunks, in his clothes, and fell promptly to sleep.

He woke the next morning with that disturbing yet somehow pleasant feeling of not knowing where the hell he was. He gathered such wits as he had, slowly realised he was in the top bunk of a moving train, and peered over. Two young Chinese men sat on the lower bunk opposite, intent on some game they were playing on a device they held between them. When they sensed his eyes on them, they looked up, smiled, and gave a little bow. He managed a weak wave back. He became aware of squeaking sounds which at first he thought were coming from their device but they were too irregular and sounded alive. He climbed gingerly down, and saw that in the bunk below him were two little balls of fur, whence the squeaks emanated. He peered in a little closer, and discovered they were tiny, curled-up puppies, one grey, one ginger. He looked at the boys and asked what the dogs were doing there. One of them reached for another device, which turned out to be a translation aid, and in a lengthy process it was explained that they were arts students in Beijing and needed money so it was quite common for their fellows to go to Moscow on the train, buy newborn puppies, and smuggle them back to China where people would pay good money. One journey would give them enough to pay their student fees to live on for a year.

The word smuggle proved quite difficult for their device to translate, and after much beeping they showed him the result on the little screen: CONTRABAND. They were nice guys and seemed to be happy that there was an English speaker on the train so they could practise. Sitting on the bottom bunk, they huddled over the device and made what conversation they could.

'We sin,' said one, looking down at this stomach and patting it. It look Steff a moment to twig.

'Thin,' he said, pointing at his mouth with his tongue between his teeth so he'd imitate him.

'Thin,' he repeated. 'You fa.'

'Fat,' said Steff, not thinking it was at all an appropriate description of him.

'Fat-uh.' Watching Steff's face closely, he mimicked the grimace.

It was striking how quickly Steff got used to life on the train, although he had hardly come prepared as his fellow travellers had. As he roamed the carriages, he saw what seemed like whole families cooking in compartments on little primus stoves, Russians in one wagon, Chinese in another. In the open carriages many had made their own little homes with curtains and brightly coloured covers. Steff ate in the spartan dining car with a handful of other Europeans, each with their own story of why they were making the journey: a clutch of backpackers and a steelworker who was spending his redundancy money on seeing the world. Steff had not even brought toilet paper, which he discovered he needed for the toilet (hole) at the snow-swept end of each carriage. Instead, he had to rely on the old copy of the Independent newspaper he had in his bag. Picking this up when he returned from a particularly perilous expedition to the loo, one of his roommates looked at the paper, consulted the device and enquired, 'Bridge card?' When Steff worked out he was asking if it had a Bridge column and indicated that he could play, the student bounced through the door and a few minutes later came back ushering in a compatriot obviously keen for a game.

How's this going to work? thought Steff. The bidding is going to be so slow. But they found a piece of paper which they rested on a suitcase on their knees and wrote their bids down: 1S for one spade, 2D for two diamonds and so on. Thus they spent many a contented hour chugging through the frozen steppes. The vastness was otherworldly. At the handful of stations they stopped at, there would be heavily swaddled babushkas standing patiently on the platform holding up their meagre wares they hoped the wealthy passengers would buy: a jar of milk, a cabbage, and one had a chicken in its feathers.

By now the dogs were stumbling around and they all took turns taking them for walks up the corridor. Steff asked what their names were, and the boys seemed intrigued by such a concept. They said he should name them. 'Ginger and Pepper,' said Steff after a moment's thought. They got him to tap the words into their translator and when he handed it back they giggled, if that was not too unmanly a word, laughed and nodded. His mind went back to Mr Zhen and Valentina in Villeneuve, when the Soviet Union and China were sworn enemies. Mr Zhen had two stock expressions: a giggle and an 'aw' with a frown. He often got them wrong:

'My father's not well.'

'Hahaha.'

'It's my birthday today.'

'Awwwww.'

They managed to get the dogs over the Mongolian border without too much trouble because they were asleep in a suitcase. Even so there was a tense moment when an alarmingly robotic border guard opened the door with her team to inspect documents and cast a hawk eye around the compartment.

That was relatively easy, said the boys after she'd gone. The real challenge would come at the Chinese border where they were ruthlessly thorough in their searches. Steff almost gulped when he imagined how that would turn out.

Mongolia was another planet again: a moonscape, with the odd huddle of yurts in the distance. Even the low-rise apartment blocks of Ulan Bator were like nothing he'd seen. They'd changed the dining car to a local one and he found the food was unidentifiable but tasty. Some kind of stews, mainly, and lots of meat dumplings. The menu said mutton, which seemed to have disappeared from supermarkets back home. The vastness and variety of the journey had opened his eyes on the world in a new way. And he saw that in all this divergence, people were really the same the globe over.

They were to approach the Chinese border late in the evening. All that day, Steff got the others to walk Ginger and Pepper up and down the corridor to tire them out so they'd sleep as they crossed. It just seemed to get them pumped up. The Chinese whispered among themselves and asked him to put them in his bag – the implication being the border guards would not bother with a European's luggage. He could see headlines with the words 'border' and 'drama' in them. He said he had a better idea. He fetched his bottle of duty-free vodka (almost empty) and mimed filling a capful and pouring it down Ginger's mouth. It was what his uncle used to do with orphaned lambs when he brought them into his grandparents' kitchen: give them a little gin, wrap them in an old blanket in a cardboard box and put it in the bottom oven of the range so they'd have a peaceful night's sleep. Another whispered huddle. The boys sat on the bottom bunk peering nervously out at the scenery and nodded simultaneously. Now was the time.

Steff performed the act. It worked. They bundled the dogs under the covers and there was no movement. The train would stop for quite some time at the border. It entered a huge shed for the chassis to be hoisted off the wheels so they could be changed for the Chinese gauge. The three waited. They heard the guards enter their carriage and search each compartment. Next door there was a huge commotion. Steff allowed himself a peek from the door, then one of the guards motioned him back with angry shouts and gestures. But he had enough time to see they were dismantling the roof panels and bringing down many well-wrapped bundles which turned out to be car parts. Other guards were summoned and the packages and people were carted off. Then it was their turn.

They searched the boys' bags thoroughly and messily, leaving them open and jumbled up. They just required Steff to unzip his and gave it a cursory glance. All was still quiet, but just as the head guard turned to leave, there was a squeak. He turned back and gave a stern, inquisitive look. One of the boys pressed buttons on the translator he held and it beeped. The guard gave a sniff, seemed satisfied and turned to go again, But there were more squeaks, of a higher pitch than the beeps. He batted the boys off the bunk, threw back the covers, and found the dogs. He picked them up and handed them to one of his minions. The boys and their bags were escorted almost ceremoniously off the train.

Steff was allowed off the train and came across the boys being held outside the customs office. He managed to have a few words with them – they'd made some progress in their week's intensive course. He asked, with the help of mime, what would happen to the dogs. They knew the word 'sell' – the guards would probably sell them and keep the money. What about you? They looked downcast, and gave the universal sign for money by rubbing their thumbs against their forefingers. A fine or possibly a bribe. Or – and here one of the boys gripped his fists in front of his face – prison. He toyed briefly – very briefly – with the idea of asking how much it would take to get them out of trouble, but then the headlines flashed up again and he sadly wished them good luck and goodbye.

The compartment was lonely without them. Even the sight of the Great Wall, as exhilarating as it was, did not do much to lift his spirits. He went on to Beijing and spent a couple of weeks there writing heavily censored cultural features. Looking back, the Trans-Siberian express was one of the favourite journeys of his life. When he got back to London, he wrote it up for Voyages to considerable acclaim. Even the doubting editor slapped him on the back.

Over the years he compiled a large repertoire of train songs which he transferred to an iPod when they came out and accompanied him on his travels. His favourites were: *Slow Train* by Flanders and Swann, an evocative in memoriam to the old rail network before Beeching wielded his axe to it; Duke Ellington's *The A Train* which immediately transported him to jazzy New York City; the wondrously wholesome Australian group The Seekers and their hit *Morningtown Ride*; the soulful *Midnight Train to Georgia* by Gladys Knight and the Pips, and *Last Train to London* by one of his favourite bands, The Electric Light Orchestra.

His job took him to the ends of the earth for many memorable adventures: to Patagonia, where he was treated as something of a hero by the locals because of his Welsh. But theirs was rather a strange version, almost Biblical, and so communication was not always smooth. His travels became something of an issue when he married Esther, later in life, and she wasn't happy for him to carry on when the children came along. She was reasonable about it, he had to admit, didn't make a great fuss and in fact set him on his new course, which was how he made his name.

'Could you do it in some other way?' she asked one night after dinner when he'd just come back from South Africa. She thought for a moment. 'How about writing travel books?'

'Travel guides are usually just where to go and what to see,' he said, not taking to the idea at all.

'Well, you could do something different – widen them out, make them deeper. More interesting.'

He knew – or thought he knew, for who can know what's really going on in someone else's mind – that in her heart of hearts she would have him stay at home permanently. The couple hardly ever fought, but they were great sulkers. Both were independent and didn't take lightly to being told what to do. Steff thought this was the deal between them, and even though he knew she was trying to see things from his point of view, he resented even this interference, as he saw it.

'You think I'm being selfish by doing my job?'

'No, but it is your priority. Sometimes I think we could become a bit more of a team as we get older.'

'Well, your job is your priority.' Esther was an architect, and would become completely absorbed when in the midst of a big project.

'Of course it is, and should be.'

'You think I'm neglecting you?'

'Stop putting words in my mouth. All I'm trying to say is when we got married, we both knew our careers were precious to us. I'm just thinking we won't have them forever. We should work on being together more. And then there's that obsession of yours with the aunt. Sometimes I feel shut out. You accuse your family of being secretive but you don't always share things with me either. Your f-e-e-l-i-n-g-s.' She drew out the word which, in her New York accent he normally loved, gave her little speech a rather unpleasant edge to his ears.

'I just don't feel the need to chatter inanely just for the sake of it.'

Both seemed to realise that things had gone far enough. Esther left the room and they avoided each other for the rest of the evening.

In his heart of hearts, Steff knew that neither of them were right or wrong. When he'd calmed down a little, he thought about her words. He also knew that he could not give up travelling altogether. It had become his way of life, finding out about the world and its peoples, trying to get into their hopes and fears, their human condition, trying to convey some good and beauty in the world.

The more he thought about it, though, the more he could see the potential of Esther's idea. He told her so the next day, after they'd spent the night hugging their respective edges of the bed. Peace and speaking terms were restored. So that's what he did, and he didn't have to travel so much. His wasn't just the kind of best beaches and hotels kind of writing; he focussed on cultural, societal and sometimes political aspects and loved cities best of all. He made this his trademark, and his books sold well. He had a light touch and drew on people's first hand stories. He always remembered Ethel's teeth.

He also remembered the Chinese boys on the train and often wondered what happened to them. His busyness left him little time for that other mystery that had for so long and so intensely absorbed him. But all that changed when his grandmother died.

12

His grandfather had died of lung cancer a few years before. He was in the Himalayas when his mother called, but he couldn't get back to Paris in time. He viewed it as one of the sacrifices of his career that he wasn't always on hand for events with his family and friends. It had to be said, though, that no tears were shed for his Papie – even his mother didn't seem upset. There'd been no bond between them, that much had been obvious, quite the contrary. Steff himself had found him difficult to get to know and impossible to love. Why was that, he wondered? He'd never discussed it with his mother, but on the train from Calais to his grandmother's funeral, he decided to try.

Hi mother had come up to London the night before and stayed with him and Esther in their flat in Maida Vale. His father, she said, had a bad case of flu and was not up to the journey. He had never set foot in that house in Conflans since Steff was a baby. Esther was too busy on a big project, designing social housing in the East End. She'd been full of profuse apologies, but Steff had brushed them aside. Really, he didn't mind. And it would be good to have some time alone with his mother.

He hadn't quite worked out her reaction to her mother's death. She'd gone on living in that house alone, and 'gone on' was the apt phrase: she was almost ninety when she died. It must have been a solitary, empty existence. After dinner, the two of them sitting in the living room nursing glasses of wine while Esther busied herself with something in the kitchen, his mother spoke of her last years.

'I did go and see her now and again. She was getting frail and I talked to her about a retirement home but she wouldn't hear of it. She just wanted to go on with the routine she'd always known. At least I managed to find a cleaner cum carer to go in daily and check she was OK. She objected to that too, but as I was paying she couldn't dismiss her. I think eventually they came to some understanding and even became a strange kind of companions, if not friends.'

Some of the old questions came back to percolate in Steff's head. Why had he always had the feeling that there was something his family had never told him about his aunt's disappearance? Why was it that they'd never shown the slightest curiosity about what happened to her? Could it be, as they claimed, that it was just because she'd turned her back on them, as they saw it? Surely, then, they would still wonder what had become of her, especially after all these years. Had she married, had a family? Were there grandchildren, nieces and nephews? Something didn't add up.

These questions and thoughts whirled around his head in a rather higgledy-piggledy fashion as the the Eurostar train whizzed through dreary countryside of Northern France under a heavy drizzle. His mother sat quietly beside him, seemingly lost in her own thoughts. It was difficult to know how to start. How could he get her to open up a little? She hadn't spoken of her feelings since she phoned him to tell him of the death. But maybe now that he was older he would be able to understand a little better, and she would realise that.

'What will you miss most about Mamie?'

He sensed his mother bristle somewhat next to him. But she seemed to consider and be prepared to answer, which she did after a moment or two.

'Well, we weren't particularly close, as you know,' she said.

I know no such thing, he thought.

'My father was always distant,' she said, rather reluctantly, he thought. 'I don't think my mother was very happy. The marriage wasn't very happy. They didn't fight or anything like that. They just didn't communicate very much. So it was quite a silent home – not a very warm one, compared to some of my friends'.'

'Is that why you left and went to London?'

'I suppose that must have come into it. But I didn't particularly think that way at the time. I'd always been good at English and wanted to go to England and with all the talk of Hitler and war, it seemed the best thing to do.'

She thought for a few seconds.

'Maybe without realising it that's partly why I started thinking about other lands, other languages. But I also believe that, just as some people are destined to stay close to home, others must stray. I'm not sure there's any rhyme or reason to it. I just had this sort of fascination with things English. Or British, I should say,' she added with a smile. 'I remember an image in a school book we had. It was of a city gent on a zebra crossing. His bowler hat had blown off his head and he was kneeling down and trying to retrieve it with his umbrella. That was the image the French had of the British then, I suppose. Very proper, well-behaved and disciplined.' She seemed lost in her reverie. 'That's changed now of course. It's all Punk and riots.'

'So you will miss her?' For some reason he wanted to hear her say it.

'Oh, yes of course,' she said, a note of resignation in her voice. 'She was my mother. Don't get me wrong, she always looked after us, fed us well, nursed us when we were ill and all those things.' There was another pause. 'I'll miss her not being there. But, after living abroad for so long, it's not the same as if I'd seen her every day.'

Steff picked up on those 'usses.' He was dying to ask further about her relationship with her sister, but felt that this was still a closed door. He didn't want to push it. He suddenly had another thought: was it at all possible that his aunt would turn up for the funeral? But how would she have heard about it? Maybe there was some unknown mutual friend she was still in touch with. Or an obituary notice somewhere. Then he got to wondering if the same thought had occurred to his mother. This was not the moment to ask, though. Perhaps something would transpire at the funeral.

It was to be held in the small church atop an outcrop high above the Seine, with burial in the local cemetery afterwards next to her father. They got a cab from Conflans Fin d"Oise station straight to the church. The rain clouds had passed and it was already sweltering on this midsummer's day. The coffin was in place before the altar steps as they went in, and as Steff had foreseen, only a handful of people in the pews. Rita and Bob were there, looking older of course, and they raised hands and gave weak condoling smiles at him. It must have been three or four years since he'd seen them and he hadn't had the thought or time to get in touch beforehand. He was glad they were there. Otherwise, there was only an elderly couple sitting behind them, an old woman near the back and a couple and two equally ancient men a few rows in front of her. Neighbours, he presumed. Maybe the two men were former railway colleagues of his grandfather. And in front of them, a younger woman, black and all in black. Even in this sombre garb she looked bubbly. She must be the sort of companion, Steff supposed. She and her mother exchanged friendly nods as they progressed with a suitably respectful pace down the aisle.

The service was as simple and short as a Catholic service can be, as there were no eulogies. What a sad end, thought Steff. His mother dabbed her eye with a lace handkerchief a couple of times, but he could see no tears.

Behind them, someone sobbed quietly. When it was over, his mother said Solange the companion had arranged for a car to follow the hearse to the cemetery. Outside there were the customary words of condolence and thanks. His mother told everyone they would be welcome to the cemetery and to the house afterwards for refreshments. No-one said much about the woman who was embarking on her last journey, apart from the usual 'she's in a better place,' or 'she's at peace.'

There were only six at the cemetery – Rita and Bob , Solange, and the elderly woman at the back.

'Who's she?' whispered Steff to his mother after the coffin had been lowered and they'd thrown soil on it. The priest was still saying prayers.

'I don't recognise her,' said his mother through tight lips, but didn't raise her eyes from the grave.

He did give the woman a good look, realising that he was in fact looking for any family likeness. He found none. The woman was tall, while his mother and her parents were short, and their faces were different shapes. He wondered then, what she was doing here.

Would she have known his aunt? He went up to her.

'We'd like you to come back to the house for some refreshment,' he said.

'Thank you. I'd like that,' said the woman. She had a sweet smile.

'How did you know my grandmother?' He said it with a smile, so it didn't sound too inquisitive.

'Well, I…'

'Excuse me. Steff, it's time to get the car to the house.'

He was annoyed at his mother's interruption, which he thought was rude, and unlike her.

'Madame…?' He looked at his new acquaintance.

'Kléber.'

'Madame Kléber is coming back for refreshments.'

'You're very welcome,' said his mother, still unsmiling.

'Would you like a lift?' said Steff

'No, I have my car, thank you.'

'And you know where the house is?'

'Oh, yes.'

In the car, Steff wanted to get to the bottom of his mother's offhand manner to Mme Kléber, but Solange was with them and he didn't want to bring it up in front of her. Instead he asked Solange conversationally, 'Do you know Mme Kléber?'

'I think I saw her at the house a couple of times, but not really to talk to much.'

'Was she a neighbour?'

'I suppose I assumed so.'

'Did my grandmother ever talk about her?'

'No-oo, I don't think I can recall that she did.'

His mother, sitting next to him, nudged him in the ribs. He realised that it was sounding a little like an interrogation. But he found Solange's answers vague, if not downright evasive. Again, he couldn't help thinking that she knew more than she was letting on. Or was he getting just a tad too obsessive?

It was a gloomy little gathering at the house: just the six of them and the priest. Everything was spick and span – Solange's work, no doubt. But it was spooky, as if there was a presence: obviously not his grandfather, who was hardly ever in the house in waking hours. He began to think that in her own quiet, buttoned-up way, his grandmother must have been something of a character. Realising suddenly that his mother wouldn't know Rita and Bob, he introduced them and badly wanted to catch up with them, but first he was determined to find out about Mme Kléber before she vanished, and went over to her where she stood by the window nursing a kir.

After a couple of preliminaries he asked her if she'd known his grandmother for long.

'Well, we moved into the street a couple of years before the war. My husband and I, that is. It was our first house. So for a while we were on nodding terms in a neighbourly way, you know, and gradually there were invitations to coffee and what have you. Not much more than that for years. But after your grandfather died, I came more often.'

Steff took a liking to her. She was soft-spoken and had a twinkle in her eye.

'And how was she, these last years?'

'Very frail. Nothing wrong with her as such, she just sort of faded away. Solange has been an angel. She couldn't have managed without her.'

'Was she happy, here alone?'

Mme Kléber gave him a quick, meaningful look. He somehow knew she'd give him an honest answer.

'Well, you know your grandmother. She wasn't what you'd call the life and soul of the party.' The phrase she used was the *boute-en-train de la bande.* 'There was a sadness there. So I couldn't describe her as happy, no.

Perhaps accepting is a better word. She was accepting of her lot.'

'Did she ever talk to you about her sadness?'

'No. She didn't open up much. She didn't complain.'

'So you remember my mother.'

'Only very vaguely. She left for England soon after we came.'

He hesitated slightly before asking, 'And my aunt Céleste? Do you remember her?' Funny how you can trust strangers almost at first sight.

'I would say that I was dimly aware of her for a short while. She wasn't here much. She was teaching in Paris. And then the war came and, well…'

'Did my grandmother ever speak of her?'

'Never.'

'No. She disappeared during the war, and the family seemed to close ranks and cast her out of their lives.'

'And they don't know why?'

'No, and they don't even seem curious. But I am. I'm trying to find out what happened to her. I know she was teaching in a school near place de la République until at least 1946.'

'And after that, no trace?'

'No trace.'

'I wish you luck. And sorry that I can't help.'

'No, it's been interesting talking to you. But if anything occurs to you about my aunt…'

'Yes, of course.'

He took her over to his mother and introduced them. She was a little more welcoming this time. He found Rita and Bob leaning against the sink sipping cognac. After hugs and a catch-up, Rita took him aside and said, 'You know, it's a strange thing but after your grandmother died I saw a woman peeking through the upstairs window of this house'

'Really? Are you sure?'

'Well, no, not a hundred per cent. In fact the first time I thought I must have dreamt it.'

'You mean it was more than once?'

'Twice, I think.'

'What did she look like?'

'Look, it was just a vague shadow behind the net curtains. Just a silhouette, really.'

'Always in the same place?'

'The same window. But she did move around a bit.'

Steff let this sink in. It was entirely possible, of course, that Céleste would have a key to the house, even after all these years. How she found out about her mother's death was another question. His thoughts raced. Could she have reconnected with her mother in her twilight years? In which case, why wasn't she at the funeral? To avoid having to confront her sister and nephew, possibly.

'If you see her again, will you let me know?'

'Yes, OK.'

Steff found it strange that Rita seemed not to grasp what a big deal this could potentially be. But, no, it was unlikely that, if it was indeed her, she'd come to the house again. It had been left to his mother, and would be put up for sale.

They were to stay in the house for the next few days.,

while his mother made the arrangements. Steff had his qualms about sleeping there, for some reason, and had suggested going to the charming little hotel near the station, but his mother wouldn't hear of it. He glanced across at her. She and Mme Kléber were chatting with something approaching empressement. They shook hands warmly, and his mother lifted her finger to the corner of her eye, as if to brush away a tear. It seemed to be the signal for the others to disperse. As they were leaving, Rita kissed him and said,' Come to dinner tonight.' There was nothing Steff would have liked better, but he said he should stay with his mother.

'An *apéro* then.

Steff knew what that meant. They'd be there for hours.

'Maybe not tonight.'

'No. Of course. But come and see us.'

The afternoon was still hot. His mother suggested a walk along the river before supper – there was plenty of cold meats, cheese and wine left. They could pick up a baguette. Even now, Steff could not see one without thinking of those long compartments in kitchen cabinets to house them. Indeed, the mere mention of the word made him glance over at the one nearest to him. Although he could never recall a baguette being in there.

They negotiated the steep, narrow path down through the garden, now rather overgrown, and found the door at the bottom with its rusted old lock holding a huge key. Neither of them had thought about having to open it, and they exchanged quizzical looks as to whether the key would turn. To the surprise of both of them, it did, easily.

It gave on to a narrow lane, and there were steps down to the path along the Seine, made of old railway sleepers and earth.

There was the whiff of a breeze by the river which was soothing and invigorating at the same time. As they strolled along, his mother began to hum softly. He recognised the tune: *Quand on S'promène au Bord de l'Eau,* sang by Jean Gabin in the 1930s. She used to sing it to him when he was young. Maybe that's what made him want to find out more about the actor. It told of workers who'd come out from the 'prison' of Paris on their day off and walk along the river, just as they were doing.

Out of the blue, his mother had a fit of sobbing. He guided her to a bench on the riverbank and put his arm around her, which she shrugged off gently. The sobs ebbed. It was still, with just the vague hum of insect life and gentle lapping of the water. Even the birds seemed to find it too hot for much activity.

'My father used to bring me here and sing that song. He loved it.' She sniffed. He grappled with what to say.

'It's nice here,' he said, thinking: is that all you can come up with? His mother continued staring at the water rolling by.

'You know, I've been thinking,' he said. 'You don't have to sell the house, do you? I mean, we could come here for holidays and walk along the river and…'

'I never want to come here again,' she said.

'What?'

'You know what you said on the train. About me being happy? Well, I wasn't. It wasn't a happy home.'

'Why not?'

'Well, you know my father was, detached, shall we say. But…there was a bit more to it than that.'

'What more?'

She took a deep breath.

'He used to hit us. Not often. But hard. And then he'd be sorry, and came to cuddle us. That was a bit too hard too.'

'You mean he…?

'I don't know.' It was almost a shout. 'I just can't remember. Maybe I've blanked it out. I just know I didn't like it. Talking to Mme Kléber brought some of it back. People around sort of knew that something was not quite right.'

'Didn't your mother do anything?

'He never did it in front of her. But I'm sure she knew. Maybe that's why she turned in on herself. He did too. He wasn't always like that. I hope he felt ashamed. And maybe that's why Céleste left and never came back.'

That was the first time he'd heard his mother say her sister's name, as far as he could recall. They sat there for a few moments watching the sun sink behind the poplar trees on the opposite bank. She let out a long sigh.

'I feel a bit better now. Thank you, Steff.'

He wasn't totally sure what she was thanking him for, but was glad and just a little proud that she'd opened up to him at long last.

The next afternoon he decided on a whim to go back to the school in Villeneuve where he'd taught some twenty years before. His mother was off seeing estate agents and notaries and whatnot about the sale of the house. Like his mother, he wouldn't miss the place. He'd only suggested that she hang on to it for some kind of comfort, clearly misplaced.

It was quite a schlepp to get there: train into St Lazare, metro line 9 across Paris, then train from the Gare de Lyon. As he walked up from the station towards the school the thought briefly struck him that he might come across some of his former pupils. He imagined them looking slightly older. But then he realised they would now probably have children of their own – grandchildren even. It sobered him.

The school was still there, recognisable but changed. It had been painted white, and a new block with a vast glass entrance had replaced the old lodge. The gates were locked, but he could see that some of the trees had been cut down. It looked more manicured, controlled. It had been renamed the Lycée Rosa Parks. And just to the right of the entrance was a plaque. He could just about make out the writing. It was a memorial to the Jewish students who'd been deported to the death camps.

His mother was pleased with the way her afternoon had gone. She'd found a nice estate agent who would take care of everything.

'What about all the furniture and stuff?

'They'll auction it all.'

'Won't that be expensive?'

'In France the buyer pays the estate agent's commission, not the vendor. Of course they'll take a cut of the auction, but I can't see what else we'd do with all this.' She waved her hand around the kitchen.

'Don't you want to take anything for keepsakes?'

'Maybe some of my mother's jewellery. There's not much. And if I spot any little piece that takes my fancy, well, yes, of course. And I hope it goes without saying that you're welcome to take whatever you like. I'll ask Solange to come over too. But as you can see the place is a bit bare of knick knacks. It's all a bit plain.'

Off the top of his head, Steff couldn't think of anything he desperately wanted. But he welcomed the chance to have a good rummage – sprwt, they'd say in Wales – in the hope that he might upturn some clues about his aunt.

He was disappointed. There was hardly anything in the way of letters, and the few photographs showed his mother as a young girl, the grandparents, and a few older ones of long-dead relatives, he assumed. He took a silver-framed picture of their wedding, just to show willing as it were, and an inlaid writing box, hardly used. Solange came and took some bedding and dining room linen. It was a disheartening task, and a sad legacy for two lives.

13

The letter arrived when Steff was in his late fifties. He picked it up slowly from the doormat, wondering at it, and shoved the other mail and newspaper under his arm. It was a cream coloured envelope with embossed lettering in the top lefthand corner: *Cabinet* and then a long name, double-barrelled. He knew it meant an office, probably lawyers. He ripped it open impatiently, then reread it to make sure he'd understood as he walked slowly into the kitchen where Esther was eating granola and listening to the news on the radio. She looked up and could obviously tell by the look on his face that the letter he was holding in his hand was something out of the ordinary.

'Well, what is it?' she asked when he didn't say anything.

'It's from my aunt's lawyers in Paris. My aunt Céleste. She's left me a small flat in the eleventh arrondissement.

'The missing aunt? Then she's been alive all this time?' Esther knew all about his long search, now abandoned if not forgotten.

'Seems so,' he said, sitting down slowly, still holding

the letter. 'They call her Madame Céleste Renault. She must have married.'

'But why did she leave it to you? How did she know where you were? How did she know you even existed?'

'I know, I know. Or rather I don't know. One mystery leads to another.' He poured himself a cup of coffee.

'Guess I'll have to go to Paris.'

'Poor you,' said Esther. 'I know, I'll come with you. We can find a nice little hotel.'

'That would be great. But what about Maman?' What, if anything, should he say to her?

For the last two or three years she'd been in a care home in Borth, over the hill from Aberystwyth. Since the death of his father, she'd becoming increasingly fragile and less able to cope. She'd put up a bit of a fight about leaving the house she'd brought him up in, but Steff and Esther thought it a mere token protest, and in the end she went willingly, coming to terms with her limitations.

He was due to make a visit anyway. He thought he'd get the train to Welshpool and hire a car, if there was such a facility there, to drive over the Cambrian Mountains and Plynlimon. He'd enjoy it.

It was a blustery autumn day. Fluffy clouds scuttled across the mountains, playing kaleidoscopic shafts of light on the slopes. He still hadn't made up his mind whether or not to broach the subject of his aunt's flat with his mother. She had her lucid moments, but then retreated into a world of her own, often a world of long ago. She would usually recognise him on sight, but eventually behave as if he wasn't there, or wasn't known to her. He'd have to play it by ear.

He went first to the old house by the castle in Aberystwyth. It had been sold two years before. He hardly recognised it: it had become shabby in latter years. Now there were new windows and the facade had been painted a pastel shade of blue. As far as he could tell, the roof had been replaced. There was a ramp up to the front door, with rails each side of it, as if someone in a wheelchair were living there. The house of his childhood had vanished and taken on a wholly different personality. He had some pangs of regret, while at the same time reflecting how intriguing it was that places could see so many different lives.

The home was on a hill overlooking the long beach of Borth, an old rectory or some such. At the front was a glassed-in veranda, and it was here that he found his mother, sitting in a wicker chair staring contentedly down to the sea. She was still elegant in her French way, still a version of her motherly self with her bobbed hair, now completely white, and expertly applied scarlet lipstick. Her mouth widened into her winsome smile.

'Steff, how lovely to see you. Have you come far?'

'From London, Maman, as usual.'

She asked about the children, as if they were still at home, although they had left years ago and had children of their own.

'Shall we have some coffee?' She'd never taken to tea, in all the years she'd lived in Wales.

'Yes, I'd like that.' She thought for a moment. 'Can you make it? I don't know how, here.'

'We'll ask one of the carers.'

Her eyes clouded over at his mention of the word. After a friendly young care assistant brought them mugs, Steff set about trying to find a clue as to how his aunt tracked him down. He decided against telling her about her sister's death, for the time being at least. Was there some mutual friend from the past who had never been mentioned? He tried to disguise his investigation as normal conversation: his mother liked talking about the past but did not usually go back to her childhood.

'I've been thinking about the house in Conflans,' he said. She looked at him quizzically. 'In avenue Foch. Did you ever keep in touch with some of your old friends?'

She stared out to sea, then smiled and said, 'Laurence.' For a second or two he was taken aback till he remembered that in France, Laurence was a girl's name, Laurent being the boy's version.

'Did you used to play with Laurence?' His mother switched to French.

'Of course. In those days we used to play in the street.'

'What did you play?'

'*Colin-maillard et marelle*,' she answered promptly.

He knew that *Colin-maillard* was blind man's buff, but was at a loss for the other game.

'How did you play *marelle*?'

'Well, you draw boxes on the pavement and number them one to ten and you have to jump on certain numbers.'

Hopscotch.

'Did you ever hear from Laurence after you came to Wales?'

'Yes, letters at first and then Christmas cards for a while.'

'Where does she live?'

'Conflans. But she must be dead now.'

He steeled himself for the next question, and decided to plunge straight in.

'Did Céleste play with Laurence too?'

The answer was a curt yes, and the smile vanished. She seemed to withdraw into herself and turned an empty gaze back to the sea.

'Are you comfortable here, Maman?'

'It's OK. Except for the camels.'

'Camels?'

'Yes. They come and sit on the lawn sometimes. Two of them.'

He thought about how to respond to this.

'I wouldn't worry about the camels if I were you.'

There was now no question about mentioning Céleste again or the Paris flat. Conversation became strained, and after a while he kissed her forehead and left. On the way out, it occurred to him briefly to ask one of the care assistants about the camels. Could it be possible that there were some in a circus or something? But he thought the better of it: it was ridiculous.

On the way back he stayed the night in an old wayside inn in Llangurig, the other side of Plynlimon. He rang Rita. After exchanging their news, he asked her if she ever knew of anyone who lived in the neighbourhood called Laurence.

'Well, it's quite a common name. Let me see… No, I don't think so. Still looking for your aunt, I assume?'

He told her about the flat she'd left him in Oberkampf.

'Great,' she said. 'Now you can come and see us more often.'

'Will do,' said Steff, 'and meanwhile maybe you could ask around to see if anyone remembers a Laurence in the street.'

'Will do.'

The notary's office was on the boulevard Richard Lenoir, just down from the Canal St Matin, on the third floor of a typically Hausmanian building. It was largely old fashioned, with a roll-top desk against the wall, wooden filing cabinets and green bankers' lamps, and a couple of flourishes of modernity. Esther and Steff sat at a glass desk opposite the young notary M Orfèvre who insisted on talking in barely adequate English even though Steff had explained he was fluent in French and Esther's was very good. They went through the deeds page by page, initialling each one at the bottom, and when they'd finished M Orfèvre poured them a tiny glass of cognac which was apparently customary on such occasions. Steff took the opportunity to ask him, in French, what he knew about the aunt.

'Very leetle,' he said.

'Did you act for her in other ways?'

'No, this was the only instruction we received.'

'Were there any other provisions in the will?'

'Not concerning you.'

With further questioning, they discovered that the aunt had given her address as a nursing home in Rouen.

That seemed to be the only information he could or would give.

As they walked up rue Oberkampf towards the flat, Steff said, 'It seemed odd that they couldn't tell us anything about her.'

'Everything about your aunt is odd,' said Esther with a smile, leaning into his shoulder. She'd mostly been supportive of his quest, if at times she couldn't hide the fact that she thought of it as an obsession. 'At least you know she lived quite a long life and thought of you.'

'Even though she never met me.'

'Well yes, that is a bit of a puzzle. But now you can stop searching for her.' There was hope in her voice.

'Yes, but I still want to know why she turned her back on her family.'

'Maybe they turned their back on her.'

'Mmm, you know, I never quite thought of it like that. But it's not how Mam and the grandparents told it.'

'That doesn't necessarily mean it happened that way.'

'No, but I also want to know why she left it to me, and even how she knew about me. Perhaps we'll find something in the flat.'

Esther gave a good-natured groan and a gentle punch on his arm. 'She clearly didn't want to leave any tracks.'

'Yes, but why?'

They'd been given the digicode to the front door. The entrance hall was much the same as he remembered it, except for new metal letter boxes on the left and the door to the old concierge's place which now seemed to have been converted into an apartment. They had the key to

Mme Renault's letterbox. Steff opened it eagerly and sifted quickly through the mail.

'All seems to be junk,' said Steff. 'I'll take it up and go through it properly later.'

The flat was on the third floor of the building in front of the courtyard. They climbed up the curly wooden staircase and their anticipation mounted with each step. As they opened the door, they looked at each other and Steff took a deep breath. Esther rubbed him on the shoulder for encouragement. It opened out into a dining room separated from the kitchen by a wooden counter. The place smelled musty and dusty. It must have been ages since anyone was there.

The kitchen reminded him vaguely of the house in Conflans, although it was about quarter of the size: a large porcelain sink and an old wooden cabinet which Steff now knew was a popular style in the 1940s and 50s called Mado. Steff opened the long double casement window, leant on the rail and peered into the street below. He could imagine doing this with a glass of wine in the early evening, watching shoppers hurrying home or piling into the bars and restaurants opposite.

Esther had wandered into the lounge through french windows and called him in.

'Not a bad size,' she said, nodding. It had the same aspect as the kitchen and again was devoid of any furniture or personal effects. Two shelved alcoves were bare of book or ornament.

'Look,' said Steff. 'Exposed beams.'

Esther looked up. 'They look really good, as old as the

building itself. The ceiling must have been really low when they were covered.'

'Yeah. It was obviously not designed for tall people.'

'And a nice parquet floor.'

Between the alcoves a door led to a tiny room with a small window that housed a single bed with no linen. At the back was the door to an equally tiny bathroom with the smallest bath either of them had ever seen. Steff took off his shoes and tried it for size. He could only sit in it with bent knees.

'The tiles will have to go,' said Esther. They were small, blue and white covering the floor and half way up the walls. They were mismatched – some had different patterns, placed randomly. Steff nodded in agreement. Esther cast her appraising architect's eyes around each room.

'We could knock…' She must have caught the look on her husband's face.

'All in good time. Let's not do anything too drastic straight off.'

'Oh, I agree,' said Esther, clearly disagreeing.

They turned their thoughts to trying to find some trace of the aunt. They made a thorough inspection of each cupboard, drawer and shelf: nothing.

'No clues here then,' said Esther. 'Hope you're not too disappointed.'

'It's as if she were never here,' said Steff.

They found a shop on the boulevard de Belleville which sold them a blow-up double mattress, a couple of pillows and two sleeping bags. They ordered a sofa bed which could be delivered the next day. On the way back down to the flat, they peered into restaurants. There was a great choice, but the one that took their fancy was L'Estaminet, which specialised in rustic cuisine from the Auvergne. They returned there for dinner once they'd set up the bed and bought a few basic provisions.

They sat outside in the evening sun. The waiter brought them menus in English, presumably because he'd heard them speaking, but Esther bridled at this and asked for the French version. She made a barfing gesture when her husband ordered *os à moelle* – bone marrow which came in little stacks of bones – and a salad with chicken gizzards. But they enjoyed themselves and the wine flowed. They talked about the future. They agreed a new bathroom was in order.

'What about a new kitchen?' asked Esther.

'Hmm, I think I'd like to keep it more or less as is. Maybe a new cooker and fridge. Small ones.'

'Fine by me.'

They spent a few days equipping the flat with bare essentials (Steff's contribution), and rugs, curtains and blinds (Esther's). In the central strip of the bvd. Richard Lenoir they came across an antiques fair and stopped to admire one stall, in particular two wicker chairs, an art deco wooden table, and an elegant escritoire with lots of little stationery drawers at the back. The stallholder came up and clearly expected them to start haggling.

'We'd love to get these,' said Steff, pointing, 'but we've got no transport.'

'Where do you live?'

'We've got a flat just up the road.'

'Tell you what, we pack up around 1400 and if you take all those pieces I'll bring them up in the van.'

'Third floor, no lift,' said Steff.

The guy looked at him. 'You've got legs and arms, haven't you?'

They quickly agreed on a sum close to the asking price, as the guy would deliver and, Steff hoped, help him carry the furniture up the stairs, which he duly did. They manoeuvred the pieces into place until they were satisfied and immediately the whole place took on a homely air.

That night Steff cooked his favourite *choucroute garnie*: he found the sauerkraut and charcuterie in a shop up the street and they dined at the candlelit table with 1664 beer. They were both exhausted after the day's exertions but looked around them contentedly. There was a second hand bookshop under the flat and they'd bought a few so the shelves didn't look so bare.

'It'll do,' said Esther, clinking her bottle with his. 'For the time being.'

'Certainly,' said Steff. 'I think we've done a damn good job.'

14

It was quite a few years before Steff got round to installing a new bathroom. He and Esther spent long weekends there three or four times a year, and friends and family visited too. They'd sometimes go out to Conflans to spend an evening with Rita and Bob. The old house next door had changed considerably but tastefully. A lot of money had clearly been spent: wooden shutters and a front door in the style of the era. Steff asked if they knew the new neighbours.

'Not to speak to,' said Rita. 'They've only been there two or three years. There was an elderly couple before that that we got on with fairly well. They didn't do much to the house.'

After much gentle cajoling from Esther, he finally spoke to a plumber friend of Bob's, Jean Paul, and together they went to Leroy Merlin to pick out a suite. Esther and he had decided to get a walk-in shower to replace the bath, slate to line the walls, and boat deck flooring. They fixed on a date for the installation, and Esther said Steff should go alone this time, so there'd be fewer bodies to get underfoot. JP arrived in his white van with the bulk of the furniture strapped to the rack. He was a jovial character, whereas his young mate Rapha uttered barely a word. He looked as if a gust of wind would blow him over, but as they trudged up around the stairs under the weight of the shower tray and toilet, it was Rapha who bore the brunt, whereas Steff could do little more than guide him.

After an affable discussion about what he wanted, Steff told JP he'd keep out of their way. The job was reckoned to take three days so Steff had arranged to go to stay with Rita and Bob for a couple of nights. He'd return on the third afternoon to check that all was OK and sort out any snagging. Just as he was about to leave, he almost jumped when Rapha opened his mouth and asked him a question.

'Where exactly are you from?'

'*Le Pays de Galles.*'

Rapha thought about this a moment. 'Is that near Bordeaux somewhere?'

'No you moron,' shouted JP from the bathroom above the sound of his hammering, 'think of rugby. France-Galles.'

'Is it a separate country from England, then?'

Steff explained.

When he opened the door late on the appointed afternoon, he was instantly relieved that there was no sound of work, but plenty of dust. JP emerged from the bathroom wiping his hands on a dirty rag.

'All done?'

'Almost. But we've still got to plumb in the toilet. I'll

come back tomorrow morning. Tonight you'll have to use a bucket.'

Steff laughed, thinking he was joking.

'I've left one in the bathroom,' said JP. 'Oh, and we found this behind that little panel in the side of the bath.' He nodded towards the table. It was a plain cardboard box with a lid, like a shoebox but slightly bigger, covered in dust.

'Oh thanks,' said Steff. His heart gave a leap. What secrets could it unlock? He was desperate to open it there and then, but JP was ushering him into the bathroom to inspect their work. Rapha was there, busy with a dustpan.

'*Bonsoir, m'sieur,*' he said, looking around as if to invite comment. JP appeared in the doorway.

Steff spent a moment or two taking it all in. There was total silence from the pair.

'It's brilliant,' he said. 'Just what I was hoping for. Better.' He meant it.

'*Royale,*' said JP in one of his trademark phrases, and even Rapha managed a smile. 'And I'll give the radiator in the bedroom *un coup de pistolet.*'

Steff poked his head around the door and looked at the object in question. It was indeed rather grubby, and Steff twigged that he meant he'd use a spray gun to spruce it up. He nodded.

He'd invited the pair to dinner at L'Estaminet. They'd done a grand job, and he was pleased when they'd eagerly accepted. They washed in the kitchen sink.

'Me and the lad have brought some going-out clothes and we'll change in the van,' said JP. 'Don't want to let the side down. Come down with us, and we can head straight off. Rapha here is getting hungry.'

The lad gave a shy, apologetic smile. The opening of the box would have to wait.

At the restaurant, Steff encouraged them to have a slap-up meal, and met no resistance: aperitifs of port, starters, mains, and cheese. The wine flowed, and there were cognacs and coffee to finish. It was a convivial evening, but half of Steff's mind was speculating on the contents of the dusty box.

Rapha wanted to know more about Wales, England and Scotland, so Steff gave him a brief history of the United Kingdom, and explained the difference between that and Great Britain.

'So Northern Ireland is part of the United Kingdom, but not part of Great Britain?' said JP. 'Hmm, never knew that. You have so many different names for your country.'

'Yes. Our passports say The United Kingdom of Great Britain and Northern Ireland.'

'Fancy.'

The evening ended with warm handshakes, and JP said he'd come around at eight in the morning to plumb in the toilet. Back in the flat, Steff pounced on the box, laid on the bed with it, and fell promptly asleep. Next morning he was woken by loud raps on the door. It was JP, slightly early. Steff was still in his clothes, the box on the bed beside him. He leapt up to let him in. He was as good as his word and it was a quick fix.

'There,' he said, flushing the toilet ceremoniously. 'All done.'

It was only after he'd left that Steff could finally open the box. He sat on the bed and took a deep breath. He wiped off the dust, and when it came to taking off the lid he paused, now nervous about what he would find. The first thing he saw was a small black and white photo of a baby. He turned it over. There was no writing on the back. Underneath were a few letters, written in an elegant hand, addressed to 'My Dearest.' No name. His eyes ran down to the signature, always the same: 'Your affectionate Lucien.' Then back up to the dateline. The first one he saw was 'Paris, September 1942.' Phrases here and there caught his eye: 'We belong together…' '…don't let this tear us apart…' '…you know why I'm doing this…' 'you know I'm right…' '…I'm doing this for France. For a better France. For the future of France…' He sorted them, only half a dozen or so in all, by date. They began in 1939, and ended with the 'future of France' letter. They were fairly short, and at first standard declarations of love: '…we'll always be together…' Then the third, dated August, took on a pleading tone. This would have been just after the fall of France, thought Steff: '…You agree with me, don't you…?' '…This has to be done…'

Staff read through them again carefully. There was nothing to suggest what that right thing was, or why the addressee should agree with him. No specifics. He looked into the box again. At the bottom was a small buff-coloured booklet. It was a membership card in the name of Lucien LaGarde to an organisation called *Action Française.* That rang a bell. A sinister bell. He had an idea, albeit only a vague one, that it was a virulently antisemitic network, active before and during the Second World War which played a vital part in the deportation of Jews to the death camps. Could that 'right thing' be connected in some way?

He stood there for a moment with the contents in his hand while he decided what to do next. He bundled the little cache into his jacket pocket and went over to the café opposite to take stock. He sat on the terrace and ordered a coffee and a croissant. Inside at the bar, in time-honoured fashion, a small man in his fifties in a blue denim blouson and cap was sipping a glass of red wine, a stiffener before work. Steff took the papers from his pocket and pored over them once more, gathering his thoughts.

The letters must have been addressed to his aunt, he reasoned. He knew she was living in the flat during the war and afterwards. They were written months apart, so maybe this LaGarde was living with her for periods and then was away somewhere, for some reason. He was a hater of the Jewish people, probably an active one. It could be that that was the 'right thing' he was trying to cajole her to agree with his views. He looked at the photo of the baby. It was in all probability, he decided, hers. Was LaGarde the father? There was no mention of it in the letters, so it was unlikely. Or at least it was unlikely to have been born before August 1942. He screwed up his eyes and peered at it. Was there a family likeness? Difficult to tell with a baby.

He stood up suddenly, his mind made up. He'd have to find out more about this *Action Française* and its role in the War. He went first to the internet café up the road to do some research about Jewish organisations and memorials. He found that the headquarters of the *Union des Déportés d'Auschwitz* was nearby in the rue Beaumarchais. He went back to the flat to have a quick shower, and loved it. The ceiling-mounted head gave the effect of a downpour, and made his skin tingle. He dashed out of the flat and stopped at the top of the stairs; he'd forgotten the cache, so he dashed back again.

The building where the UDA was housed looked like a standard apartment building from the outside, rather a posh one, and he went past it at first but checked the number and retraced his steps. The doors were of decorative wrought ironwork backed in glass. The only sign that confirmed he was in the right place was a small plaque above one of the brass doorbell panels which said simply UDA. He pressed it and waited. He pressed it again and waited. He pressed it for a third time and waited longer. There was no answer. At the end of the entrance he could see a woman talking on her phone, walking to and fro. He tried to attract her attention by rapping loudly on the door, but she was unable or unwilling to take any notice. He looked up the UDA's phone number which he'd jotted down. There was no response to this either. Strange, he thought, but then it struck him that it was August, when the city largely shut down for the summer getaway. He spent a minute or two pondering his next steps. He decided on the Bibliotèque Nationale, which he'd never visited. Every book published in France, he'd heard, was there.

The new library was on the Left Bank of the Seine: four glass towers shaped like open books on the corners of a huge square. He'd seen pictures and unless someone had pointed this out, he wouldn't have twigged. When he emerged from the metro station, and eventually found the main entrance, he was even less impressed. They looked like everyday tower blocks. If someone had to tell you what a building represented, what was the point? Esther and he often had discussions along these lines. Paris, amidst the uniform elegance of its avenues and boulevards, he reflected, occasionally suffered from howlers. Look at the world's landmark buildings that speak for themselves, or sing in the case of the Sydney Opera House. One glance at a cheap postcard would tell you it was built for performance, let alone magically convey giant sails in the harbour. No-one had to point this out. Sometimes he wondered if the patina of age lent a certain majesty to commonplace structures. Esther contended this was the case with London, which she described as a magnificent mess. Her native Manhattan, she would say, had a synthesis all of its own, although when they visited she preferred what she termed Old New York: early grand buildings which had something of the gothic about them. Was this how it earned its nickname Gotham City? He would have to tell Esther of his impressions, he reminded himself, as he searched at length for the reception at the lower level in the middle of the square. They were not favourable. But on the windswept terrace overlooking the Seine there were groups of young people skateboarding, rapping and breakdancing (if that was the right term – they stayed upright doing fancy twirls) – and a couple boxing. At least the library was serving some purpose to the local youth.

He went up and down the same long escalators a couple of times before he eventually found another entrance and reception desk. He asked for books about the deportations of Jews from France, and was told to go to a room J on the same level, but there they told him to go to another room – he'd need to take the lift. He found one, and assumed he'd be going up into one of the towers but when he pressed the button as advised it took him down a couple of floors. He made his way to a long gallery with a table stretching down the middle where people, mainly young, were staring worriedly at laptops. A couple of them were asleep, their heads on folded arms.

He went up to the information desk and stated his requirements. The youngish bearded guy sighed as if it was a troublesome request and started tapping on his keyboard. After a long silence, he sighed again and reached for a large arch lever file and started thumbing through that. Eventually he said 'Ah. Yes, Follow me.'

So much for information systems, thought Steff. He remembered a time when librarians would know exactly where to find books. We are losing knowledge, he couldn't help concluding, and we don't even realise it. He was led up an aisle of shelves and his guide circled his index finger vaguely at two.

'Is that all there is?' said Steff.

'*Oui*,' was the firm reply.

He'd been told that you ordered all the books you wanted and they were delivered by some kind of electronic conveyor to your desk. Was he missing something? He guessed he had to make do with what was before him.

There weren't a huge amount that seemed useful. Most of the books were about general European deportations, with only three or four specifically dealing with Paris or France. He noticed with astonishment that underneath were another two shelves of holocaust denial books. Ignoring those, he picked out the most relevant ones and found a seat at the end of the long desk and started to read under the light of the individual lamp. The first thing he learned was that the accepted term in France seemed to be *Shoah*, whereas he would have said *holocauste*. The Hebrew word referred specifically to the extermination of Jews. The most informative and descriptive book was *La Grande Rafle du Vel d'Hiv* by Claude Lévy and Paul Tillard, published more than twenty years after the end of the War in 1967. This must be the one his lecturer Anne told him was coming out all those years ago. He spent the afternoon making notes on this and a couple of others. He was astounded and horrified by what he read.

15

He later came to see this tortuous path to find information about Jewish deportations from France as some kind of metaphor for the veil of secrecy that had surrounded French involvement for so long. He could well understand that it was a cause of shame, guilt and even denial when the truth started to trickle out. It was true, of course, that during the war Nazi censorship would have stifled all news of the round-ups, the internment camps, and certainly the death camps. It took the Lévy Taillard book years later for the story to start emerging, and then a further thirty years for a state acknowledgment and apology in President Chirac's speech in 1995 after years of equivocation by French leaders about the country's role in the round-ups and deportations.

Little wonder then that his knowledge of them was so scant. What brought it all home to him, as he read on, was that one of two main round-ups in July 1942 was in the 11th arrondissement, where their flat was.

Most Jewish men had already been rounded up and sent to a newly-built housing estate at Drancy, northern

Paris, which had been requisitioned by the Nazis as an internment camp before deportation. Since the occupation, Jews were already banned from public places in the capital, from restaurants and bars, and were subject to an early evening curfew. It made a sobering contrast with one of his favourite pastimes at the Oberkampf flat – leaning over the railing of the kitchen window with a glass of wine and watching the world go by: friends meeting up, having a drink on a terrace, enjoying the simple pleasures of life.

For a time it was generally thought that women and children would be safe. In July 1942, all that changed. In the early hours doors on their flats were banged, they were loaded into buses and taken to the Vel D'Hiv, a velodrome in the east of the city. As word spread, some women took their children by the hand and jumped to their death out of windows. In the velodrome conditions were atrocious. There was barely any food or water as the families waited on the ground and in the stands until they were taken to Drancy. The lack of adequate sanitation added to the horror. Some of the old and sick died and were left where they were. Amid the screams and howls of the living, more than one woman hurled herself from the upper tiers to end it all.

One name kept cropping up: Louis Darquier, who later added the aristocratic de Pellepoix to his name in his tireless quest to aggrandise himself. He'd been a Paris city councillor in the 1930s, and in April 1942 became Head of the Commission on Jewish Questions. Equally tirelessly, he organised the transportation of Jews from all over France, even from the supposedly exempt region of the collaborationist Vichy regime in the South, under the authoritarian Marshal Pétain.

He found out that *Action Française* was originally a far-right monarchist movement and in the 1930s started aligning itself with the nascent Fascism. Through its newspaper of the same name it had fuelled violent antisemitism. After the war Darquier fled to Spain. In 1947 he was sentenced to death *in absentia*, but lived on there till his 80s. He would have felt at home in General Franco's regime. In a newspaper interview given a few years before his death, he asserted that the Nazi gas chambers were not to exterminate humans, but lice. As he was reading more about him, another name popped up: Lucien LaGarde. He wrote hysterical, poisonous propaganda for the newspaper – the Jewish menace to the French way of life and so on. That could explain the letters to the aunt, thought Steff, and possibly why they stopped soon after the round-ups. He hoped with all his heart that she objected to LaGarde's views and activities. She would of course have had no way of knowing the extent and end of the round-ups at the time. Surely she would have learnt, maybe in dribs and drabs, in the aftermath. In which case, why would she have kept his letters and membership card? Maybe in her own mind, she was burying them. Was she also hoping that one day they would be found? By him? Is that why she left him the flat? All these questions and no answers. Now, all this would have to remain mere speculation.

On the internet, he found the text of Chirac's official apology, just two months after he'd taken office. 'These dark hours forever sully our history and are an insult to our past and our traditions,' he said. 'Yes, the criminal folly of the occupiers was seconded by the French, by the French state.' He'd never liked Chirac, and certainly Rita and Bob used almost to spit his name, but credit where it's due, he supposed.

He sat at the desk for some time, letting all this sink in. He decided he needed a stiff drink. As he made his way towards the footbridge over the river, he was grateful to the singers and dancers for providing some degree of normalcy after the world of horrors he'd entered. He was feeling...what was he feeling? Punch drunk, was the phrase that came to mind, although it seemed somewhat frivolous. Walking along the embankment in the warm evening sun, he marvelled anew at the beauty of the city but saw it through new eyes, now acutely aware that it harboured dark secrets. He found a café and had a couple of large Bloody Marys on the terrace. Fortified, he proceeded to the memorial on the site of an old morgue at the tip of the Notre Dame island. It didn't look much at first sight but steps led down to sombre softly-lit underground corridors, their walls lined with countless names of the deported. It reminded him of Berlin's memorial, the labyrinthine blocks of stone which gave the feeling of enclosure and oppression. In the small exhibition space, there was only one photograph of the infamous Vel d'Hiv, and even though it was black and white the buses lined up in the rainswept street in the early morning gloom were recognisably the two-tone vehicles you saw today. The most moving of all, he found, were pencil etchings of the first arrivals there, when children thought it was a huge adventure and were trying to play hide and seek with the gendarmes, who of course were just trying to catch them to restrain them.

From there his strange, forlorn odyssey took him up to the lycée where his aunt had taught. On the outside there was now a newish looking plaque with the names of all the pupils who'd been deported, some thirty in all. As he went back to the flat he couldn't help looking up at windows of the apartment buildings and thinking, 'They might well have lived here…there…that might have been the children's bedroom.' He bought bread, ham, cheese and wine and flopped down on his bed, exhausted, to eat them. He summoned up the energy to call Esther to tell her: he had to share with someone.

First she asked about the bathroom. 'It's great,' he said. 'Turned out just like we imagined it. But I want to tell you what I've found out about the aunt and her lover.'

She listened patiently. He heard her light a cigarette and take a deep drag.

When he'd finished, she said, 'My God. The City of Light, huh? There sure were days of darkness.'

'And to think it happened on our doorstep.'

'Mmm. It reminds me of that time we were in Berlin, and went to exhibitions in the Reichstag and the DDR Museum. There were groups of schoolchildren being shown around. You said that history lessons can't be much fun for German kids. But at least they were learning about their past.'

'Yeah. I was thinking, next time we're over, I'd like to visit Drancy, where the internment camp was. There's a museum there, and apparently people live in the apartments.'

'Yes, I'd like that. Well, you know what I mean.'

There was another long inhalation of smoke.

'What you're saying about your aunt and this LaGarde guy does make some sort of sense. I'd say from what you've told me that she did not approve of his antisemitic activities. Even if there was no media coverage of the round-ups, surely there would have been talk. There must have been eyewitnesses. God, she may have seen one of those poor women jumping out of the window. Or even known one of them. Or knew others that disappeared.'

'Yup, sadly we'll probably never know.'

'And there's a new mystery now.'

'What's that?'

'What about the baby?'

'Of course. What about the baby.'

16

At first they thought they must be in the wrong place. They'd got off the bus and followed the map on Steff's phone and what they came to was an ordinary looking if bleak and shabby housing estate in the northern Paris suburbs. But as they turned a corner he recognised it immediately: a huge U-shaped block of flats five storeys high. It had hardly changed from the old photos he'd seen of the internment: it sent tingles down his spine. At the opening of the U was a solitary cattle wagon on rails, so that cleared up the matter. Even though Steff knew that it was still inhabited, it seemed unbelievable that people still lived there, going about their everyday lives. But then, they had to live somewhere, he supposed.

'So how exactly did this become an internment camp?' asked Esther as they walked around the inside of the U.

'It had just been built as one of so-called *cités jardins* that were being put up for social housing.'

'There's a euphemism for you,' said Esther, looking around her.

'Indeed. But it hadn't been fitted out yet, so the Nazis requisitioned it as a holding camp for deportations to Auschwitz.'

'And you said there's a museum here?'

'The *Memorial de la Shoah*.'

They walked right around the block but could find nothing other than entrances to flats. One of the main hobbies of its residents, of the young male ones at least, seemed to be tinkering with their cars. Steff approached one of them and asked about the museum. The guy looked vaguely hostile at first, but then he straightened up from his inspection of the engine and pointed with a spanner.

'Yes, over the road, by the lights.'

Thanking him, Steff wondered again about the inhabitants' attitudes to living in such a place. He'd even doubted that the young man would know about the museum.

The building was modern, white and boxy. The room they entered was the same, mostly taken up with a huge white model of the original Drancy. They took a lift to the third floor where arrows pointed to the main exhibition and guided tours. Here a young woman told them a talk was about to start in the basement, but it was for schools. They shrugged at each other and took the lift back down to the basement. They were soon glad they did: the young guide was engaging and clear, holding the attention of about twenty twelve year-olds. She told the story of Auschwitz survivor Ginette Kolinka, who worked on her family's market stall in Avignon. She returned home one afternoon to find German and French police in the flat.

They were all promptly arrested, separated, and Ginette was taken to prison in Marseille for two weeks, and then by train to Drancy and on to Auschwitz.

For years after her miraculous return to Paris, Ginette spoke not a word of her ordeal, writing later that no words could describe what she'd seen and been through. But then one day, continued the guide in the manner of one reading a gripping bedtime story, she allowed herself to be interviewed by Stephen Spielberg when he was researching *Schindler's List*. After that, she hardly stopped speaking and writing about those dark days: she now saw it as her job to tell the world.

'And who do you think were the guards at the internment camp at Drancy?' she asked the class.

'The Germans,' said a boy promptly, as if stating a simple matter of fact.

'No. It was the French police.'

It was the first time Steff had heard a French person stating this so categorically. He and Esther exchanged knowing looks. They helped themselves to the coffee and cake that was laid on, and then made their way back up to the third floor for the exhibition. There were many others' stories to follow, photos and films, and maps showing the routes of the deportations from all over France and out of it. As he sat listening to the audioguide commentary, he was ashamed that he found himself almost nodding off a couple of times and when he looked across at Esther her head was drooping too. It was appalling how quickly one tired of human suffering. The plain fact was the mind could not begin to encompass the stories of all the thousands of men, women and children who were sent from France and the millions all told. The plight of one could be more affecting than that of the countless. It was exhausting.

When they left they both agreed they needed a drink but didn't want to linger there. They went back to Oberkampf and made straight for their favourite café opposite the flat, the *Charbons et Vins*. It was so named, someone once told Steff, because during the First World War, certain cafés were subsidised by the state for life's essentials, in this case coal and wine. Good to get your priorities right. It could be from a film set: marble tables, old mirrors lining the walls, leather booths with brass rails atop.

After they'd ordered wine and taken their first gulp, Esther asked, 'How much did you know about the French deportations before?'

'Well, not much at all, really, until I started looking into it. I remember my lecturer at uni saying something which put me on to it.'

'It's astounding to think that this happened in our parents' lifetime. Especially your mother's, although she escaped.'

'Yeah. I wonder now, how much she could see coming when she left just before the war. Never really got to the bottom of that with her.'

'And your aunt, of course.'

'And a lot of it happened right here, in this neighbourhood.'

'Yup, quite a neighbourhood.'

It was also the early stomping ground of Edith Piaf who was accused of collaborating with the Germans during the war. The day before they'd been to see the little flat where she'd lived just up the road in rue Crespin du Gast, now a museum. They'd had to ring to make an appointment, and were met by a small elderly gent who reminded Steff of the family retainer who seemed to be a regular feature in black and white films set in big country houses. It was an unusual building for that part of the city: red brick with cream coloured plaster surrounds on the windows. As he took them through the lobby to the courtyard and then up to the third floor of the back wing, he informed them that he did this voluntarily (so they felt obliged to give him a tip afterwards). There wasn't a great deal to see in the two rooms, apart from posters, LPs and singles, and photographs. The most striking item was the famous little black dress on a dummy. She was extraordinarily tiny.

'To think that voice came from that frame,' said Esther.

The retainer pointed to a framed photo on the wall of Piaf dwarfed by a throng of soldiers.

'At first stars like her were allowed to entertain in prisoner of war camps in Germany,' he said. 'She insisted that she would only accept the invitation if French Jews were allowed in the concerts. Eventually the Germans agreed. She always made a point of having her photo taken like this, so you could see all their faces clearly. They could be used to make false identity papers if they escaped. She smuggled them in the next time she went.'

'Some people accused her of being a collaborator,' said Steff.

The old man looked affronted.

'They said that about a lot of people who stayed in Paris,' he said. 'They didn't know what they were talking about. Yes, she might have hobnobbed with German officers, but she knew what she was doing. She saw her job as singing, as lifting people's spirits, and by God she did. That's how she got the invites to perform in Germany.'

Here he gave a typical Gallic shrug.

'*On fait ce-qu'on peut.* And doing that with the photos. Remember, no-one in the city knew what we know now. And ultimately she was completely exonerated from any collaboration.'

Steff thanked him for the explanation, said he understood, and gave him a handsome tip.

'Did you know that about Piaf and the fake ID?' he asked his wife as they walked through the courtyard. She was a passionate fan, and had read almost everything she could get her hands on.

'Mmm, yes, now I come to think about it, that's fairly well documented.'

On the way back down rue Oberkampf, he looked up at the windows of the apartment blocks and said, 'I wonder if she did know about the round-up?'

Esther looked up too. 'Or did she even witness one of those poor, poor women jumping out of the window with her children?'

'Doubt it. The round-ups were at daybreak. She'd have been sleeping off the night before, or more likely carrying on carousing. Still, word must have got around. She'd have her ear to the ground. As the man said, o*n fait ce-qu'on peut*. But I suppose that must remain pure speculation.'

'Yes,' said Esther.'Like your aunt.'

Steff nodded.

Now, in the *Charbons et Vins*, Esther sprang a surprise on him.

'What do you want to do with the flat?'

'I think it's alright as it is. We've got it as we like it, haven't we?'

'Oh yes. But I was wondering…have you ever felt uncomfortable there?'

'Well, no. Not until now, anyway. Why?'

'Because that antisemitic fascist bastard lived there.'

'Nooo…,' Steph examined his feelings. 'I suppose to me, it was just my aunt's flat. I'd spent enough time trying to find it.' He paused for a sip. 'When you think about it, a lot of the flats around here would have dark pasts, where there was something bad, something evil. Around the whole of the city. The whole of the world.'

'Mmm,' said Esther. 'I guess what I'm really getting at is, how do you want to leave it? In your will, I mean.'

'Aah. Well, under French law it goes to you. I can't leave it to a cats' home or anything daft like that. And in all probability I'll go first.' He sipped his wine. 'Are we having one of our mercifully rare morbid conversations?'

'That's what I'm talking about. It would come to me. And I don't want it.'

'What?' He was startled by this statement. And he resented it.

'I don't want the responsibility, Steff. Don't you see? I wouldn't know what to do with it. Your aunt left it to you, probably for a reason. It's been a big part of your life. I want us both to decide together. Sell it, I think, would be for the best.'

Steff took a moment to consider.

'What about the children?'

'Neither of them want it. I've talked to them. They think like me. You should have your say. It shouldn't be left to chance.'

He could see the logic. He'd always admired his wife's New Yorker directness. She could manage him.

'OK,' he said, somewhat reluctantly. 'We'll sell. Now let's order some supper.'

17

Steff felt old age creeping up on him, or more accurately, rushing in with break-neck speed. It began to cause him real concern one time when he came back from Venice. They'd rented flats in Dorsoduro for the last three years. It was an ideal place for both of them: Esther with her architect's eye also loved swimming off the Lido; Steff, as a travel writer, loved exploring off the beaten track – places such as the Armenian monastery were Byron spent months translating their bible into English, and the almost deserted island of Torcello where mainlanders first fled invaders and started building their houses on sticks in the lagoon.

This time, Esther had left a couple of days before him as she was called back to London to fix some snagging on a library she'd designed in the East End. He'd taken her to the airport in a speedboat taxi, feeling just slightly guilty that he wanted to see out the term of their booking at the flat. On the last day, in a somewhat reckless frame of mind, he'd had two Bloody Marys at Harry's Bar and one outside the famed Gran Caffè Chioggia in St Mark's Square. The white-jacketed waiter brought all the ingredients to his table on a silver tray, along with small bowls of olives, crisps and ice, and mixed them to his liking. Whether the cocktails had anything to do with what he experienced when he was walking from the tube to their flat, was a matter of conjecture. It was just a slight incline, but he had to stop five times to get his breath back. He had only his trusty leather travel bag over his shoulder, and he'd lugged that all over the world, but when he got out of the lift he had to tarry a full few minutes to be able to present his usual self to Esther.

The next morning, when she was beavering away over her drawing board in the studio, he took a good look at himself in the bedroom mirror. He didn't like what he saw. And with his new perspective, admitted now that there was quite a bulge over his trouser waistband when he'd managed to squeeze it in. This must have been growing for some time without him noticing. He'd had a clear sign, he had to concede. He didn't want to become a wheezy old man whose travels were curtailed by his health. He'd have to change his lifestyle, which he was loathe to do. He loved his wine and food too much: not sweet things – he was a confirmed carnivore who adored charcuterie and cheese. He thought of Esther, still as svelte as when he'd first met her, seemingly without any effort on her part.

He'd picked up a few tricks from past periods of dieting, which he'd embark on when his trousers got too tight. One bonus was that lack of a sweet tooth, although if a plate of biscuits was put in front of him he would scoff the lot: he ascribed it to the irresistible combination of sugar and fat. He remembered seeing a documentary about experiments on mice: if they were fed sugar they'd eventually stop; if they were fed fat they'd eventually stop; but if they were fed a mixture of the two they'd just go on eating. He couldn't recall what happened to the mice then. He was sure they hadn't shown one exploding.

He rejected what he thought of as fad, gimmicky diets and relied solely on counting calories. He found a whole raft of substitutes which would vastly reduce his intake. Instead of bacon, for example, he'd drop two or three slices of prosciutto in the frying pan for a matter of seconds. He could have a good plate of that with eggs. In the same vein, water biscuits replaced bread, he used light cream cheese instead of butter, bresaola and not salami, and so on. He turned away from pies, pasties and sausage rolls and found ways of jazzing up lean cuts of meat with herbs and spices so taste buds were satisfied.

He'd never had much time for salads. He'd been conditioned, perhaps, by those of his Auntie Blod, served with tedious regularity for tea on Sundays. They were made up of chopped lettuce in a wide cut-glass bowl, topped with concentric circles of sliced tomatoes, cucumbers and hard-boiled eggs. It was supposed to be consumed with dollops of salad cream, which Steff detested and longed for his mother's homemade mayonnaise. Now he composed his own hearty versions with all the things he liked: rocket, avocado, asparagus, herbs, seeds and nuts.

Esther initially viewed this new regime with a mixture of bemusement and disdain, she who never had to worry about what she ate. She was particularly scornful of what became his signature trick of five course meals: a bowl of miso soup (next to no calories), chicken fillet with greens, salad, small piece of fruit and a handful of almonds. From soup to nuts, as Americans said when they meant the whole kit and caboodle. Worked for him. Steff was the head chef of the marriage, at least when it came to main courses, so he could allow her less stringent fare – not that she was a big eater. She liked baking, and so between them they managed like the Jack Spratts. Now she had to adapt too, doing inventive things with fruit and low fat Greek yoghurt. She enjoyed teasing Steff about the almost fanatical way he weighed himself. It had to be in the morning when he'd had nil by mouth, been to the toilet, and had nothing to eat after an early dinner the night before. She'd holler through the bathroom door, 'Remember to shave and cut your toenails first.'

He found it easier than he'd dreaded, with this motivation propelling him. He contemplated a more sedentary life-style bereft of adventure with cold horror. This time he got into a groove. He could do without wine in the week as long as he allowed himself some on Fridays and Saturdays, looking forward to it all the more. And for social engagements he'd limit himself to vodka and slimline tonic: he'd worked out that he could have four of them to one large glass of Malbec.

The pounds slid off, quite quickly to begin with. But he knew it would get harder and that exercise was called for. He took up swimming again – there was a magnificent art deco pool just down the road in Maida Vale, now restored. The first time he went he could barely manage ten lengths before he was out of puff. But he persisted, and the next time it was twenty, then thirty and up to fifty, which took him an hour. He got used to the regulars, mostly elderly. They got in free as it was council run. In his head he gave them names. There was the Splasher, who threw up fountains of water with arms and legs. The Slapper hit the water with the palms of his hands with resounding thwacks. Steff was no Michael Phelps, but he was sure it wasn't supposed to be like that. Surely the hands should enter the water like arrows, with pointed fingers? The Waver did back stroke with arms flailing wildly and at first he thought she was in trouble and seeking help. He soon realised she was swimming, not drowning. The one he found somewhat spooky was a woman who wore black cap and goggles and had one of those floaty foam tubes, yellow, sticking up from under her arms. As she came down the lane towards him, he was put in mind of a giant mutant wasp coming in for the kill.

He found his time in the baths relaxing, leaving his phone at home so there were no distractions in this new world littered with technology. He could work out problems that niggled him as he swam up and down, up and down. He was entertained by the effect on the swathes of the light playing from the windows in the arched ceiling. They would create rippling strips of white, shades of grey and electric blue above the wavering black lane lines at the bottom of the pool. He thought of it as kaleidoscopic art.

He soon began to feel much better, both physically and mentally. He even began pitching ideas at editors, with some success. He now realised, in his new state of heightened self-awareness, that he'd been in a rather dark place for some time. He'd had troubling thoughts about guns. They'd crop up suddenly when images of some incident in his past that he now regretted played in his mind. It could be the most trifling of things, if he'd said the wrong thing or stayed silent when he should have spoken up. He'd fire an imaginary pistol, sometimes in the air, sometimes at someone whom he'd wronged or had wronged him, and occasionally he'd turn it on himself. He could feel anxious about the slightest problem. He knew that as you got older, your anxiety dial tended to head towards maximum. He'd always prided himself on his easy-going attitude, had cultivated it throughout his years of travel, jumping on trains and planes at the last minute without the merest qualm. He knew deep down that he should talk to someone about this. He'd been brought up to keep his troubles to himself: to open up was seen as weakness. He thought about his grandparents in Conflans, how closed-in on themselves they'd been, how *renfermés*. Things were changing. You saw footballers, celebrities and even the royals talk about mental health on TV, about how important it was to find someone who'd listen. It was the first step on the road to recovery.

In his case, it was only when he started to feel something near his old self again that he could share his worries with Esther, over dinner one night when they usually had any heart-to-heart. He'd allowed himself two or three glasses of wine to oil the cogs, as it were. She listened patiently, not telling him to do this or that, and almost immediately he felt his load was lightened, that he was unburdened.

'I knew there was something wrong for the past few months,' she said. 'I tried to get you to talk, but it seemed to have the opposite effect. You'd withdraw further into yourself.'

He gave an apologetic smile and shrug. 'My old habits died hard.'

'I put it down to a certain lack of purpose you might have had – you know, in your semi-retirement.'

Steff acknowledged that he'd become somehow lost as his career dwindled. He was still asked to appear on TV and radio as a travel expert, but the invitations were becoming rarer, and he knew he would usually be the last resort. Producers would want someone who was not male, pale and stale as the parlance now went. He understood this. It was the natural order of things. He still wrote the odd feature for various papers and magazines, and even toyed with a new book, but while ideas sometimes whirled around in his mind, they never solidified.

'I also at times wondered…,' and here Esther paused slightly as if to have a good run up at what she was going to say… 'if your obsession had something to do with it too.'

His obsession was a sort of shorthand for the question of the aunt.

'You really think so?'

'I don't know. Do you?'

'I don't know either.'

'Because that's unfinished business, isn't it?'

'I suppose it is, in a way.'

It was that same evening, when he went to check on emails in his end of the study, that he saw the Facebook message.

18

Steff had an increasingly dim view of social media, or antisocial media as he started to call it, which he thought of as witty and original until he realised it wasn't. He tried to tell himself that they had their uses – for uniting isolated and vulnerable people who needed support, for example. For campaigning. Yes, there were benefits, but they were vastly outweighed in his mind by the hate, extremism and criminality that spewed forth. He tended to avoid them wherever possible. He was acutely aware that he should be using all platforms which would help his profile, as people kept telling him he should, to promote his work. But he found the whole rigmarole both tedious and stressful at the same time and so was bad at it.

It was a lucky chance then that he saw the email that night, and even more unusual that he opened it. He often deleted emails if he didn't recognise the sender, as he ignored phone calls with no name. But this one jumped out at him – the sender appeared to be French. The surname didn't mean anything to him, but a place name jumped out at him. It was in the language of his mother and was to the point. It said:

> *Please forgive me for contacting you out of the blue like this. My name is Sebastien Gagneux and I believe we may have a connection. My mother was born in Conflans-Sainte-Honorine, near Paris. Please could you send me your birthdate and that of your mother and I'll give you more information. I just need to be sure that you're the person I'm looking for. Thank you.*

Steff read it over a couple of times as he tried to decide what to make of it. Someone who knew his family, perhaps. How did they find him? He printed it out and took it upstairs where Esther was already asleep. She hated being woken up but he was sure this was reason enough.

'Hmm?' she said as he shook her.

'Sorry to wake you, but have a look at this. What do you make of it?'

Esther rolled over sleepily, her grumpy face on, and snatched the paper.

'It could be some kind of scam,' she said, and rolled back over.

'But it could be the missing link…someone who knew my aunt. I've always thought there must be someone in the street, in the area, who knew my mother and her sister.'

'Well, don't give them our address or anything like that. Bank details and so on.'

'Of course not.'

He went back down to the study and typed a reply, providing the information requested and saying he'd be interested in hearing more about their connection. He pressed the send button with a sense of purpose.

He tossed and turned for quite a while as he thought of possibilities. And suddenly it came to him. His heart raced. He couldn't wait to tell Esther. As daylight came, he lay watching her, willing her to wake. When she did, he said as gently as he could, 'Remember that email I showed you last night?'

'Vaguely.'

'I've had an idea who sent it?'

'Well…who?'

'The baby.'

'A baby sent it?'

'Céleste's baby.'

Esther was suddenly alert. She sat up.

'Of course. I should have figured that out last night. Must have been too sleepy. But why now?'

'Maybe he's only just worked out how to find me. They say you can find anyone these days.'

'Have you replied?'

'Yes, before I came to bed.'

He checked his phone. No reply from the French address. Throughout the day his fingers hovered over his phone, but none came. Perhaps this Sebastien was at work: he would do it this evening. Steff got annoyed when people expected immediate replies to emails, but when the tables were turned he could see that this instant medium carried great expectations. None came that evening either. He was tempted to send off an inquiry, but managed to contain himself. It was Esther who gave a possible scenario: maybe the dates Steff had given had proved that he was not the person this Sebastien was looking for. She was not being helpful, thought Steff. Practical, but not helpful. Perhaps she was right – the next day went by with no email. At least he could have the courtesy to tell me, Steff began to think.

But on the third day, as he sat at his computer desk seemingly reading the paper but surreptitiously eyeing the screen, this pinged up:

> *I'm sorry I've taken a little while to get back*
> *to you, but I needed to find the right way to*
> *say this. From the information you've provided,*
> *I have to tell you that in all probability we are*
> *cousins. My mother was born Céleste Dujardin*
> *in Conflans, and she had a younger sister Camille*
> *who was born on the date you gave. That cannot*
> *be mere coincidence, wouldn't you agree? If you*
> *do, let me know, and maybe we could arrange a*
> *phone call in two or three days once we've let*
> *it all sink in and worked out what we want to say*
> *to each other and ask. There's a lot to catch up on -*
> *too much for emails.*

This time Steff didn't need to read it again. He let out a strange sound, a long blend of yay and yes. Esther turned around from her drawing board and said, 'What?'

'It's the baby. It's him. It's Céleste's son. My cousin.'

'My God. The final chapter.'

They were both silent for some moments, neither knowing what to say.

'What are you going to do?'

'I'm going swimming.'

'Ah?'

'And think about all the questions I'll have for him.'

Steff noticed a bounce in his steps as he walked to the pool. He was conscious of taking deep breaths of the late summer air, and enjoying it. Once he was in the water, all the things he wanted to know came flooding out. When he got home he wrote them down, went over them with Esther, at his desk in the study.

She leant over him, her hand on his shoulder, as she she silently perused his questions.

'Hmm,' she said.

'Hmm, what?'

'You haven't asked him why now.'

'Why now? Why does it matter? Isn't it enough that it just, well, happened as it has?'

'Might hold the key.'

'Don't see how.'

'Give it a shot.'

'OK-ee.'

'Coffee?'

'Huh, yeah, thanks.'

And as she left the room, she threw back over her shoulder, 'And get him to send a pic.'

For some reason, that thought had never entered his head. It came a few days later, and they both pored over it. It was of a well-dressed and groomed man with short white hair and tortoiseshell glasses. Yes, there was a likeness, not striking, but discernible if you were looking for it. With it came swapped snippets of information. He'd been a lecturer in French literature. He was married with children and grandchildren but Steff, and he assumed his cousin too, was keeping so much back until they could meet in the flesh. For his part he learnt that Sebastien had been adopted as a baby, to a couple in Normandy, and only found out about and then traced and found his birth mother when she was nearing death.

They fixed the date for their meeting in Paris a month or two hence. Steff badly wanted Esther to go with him, but she put her foot down, and a firm foot it was.

'No, you go alone, darling. It's your quest, your holy grail.'

He had to readjust his thoughts for a moment.

'Have I been that obsessed, that thoughtless to you, that selfish?'

Esther gave a long sigh to give herself the time to think, to be honest with him without hurting him, which was the last thing she wanted.

'I always knew it was something you had to find out, and you wouldn't have got anywhere without being single-minded about it.'

'Did you feel it came before you?'

She went over to the sofa, sat next to him and put her arms around him.

'Never second best. Just had to take a back seat sometimes.' She kissed him.

Steff and his cousin agreed to meet in Paris in the middle of November. He'd been invited to stay with him and his wife who had a flat near the Bastille, but Steff somehow thought it would be better if he stayed in Oberkampf – he'd never been able to bring himself to sell it. There were certain things he wanted to do, and he decided to go over there a few days before the rendezvous. At the start of the year, he'd followed the attack on the Charlie Hebdo offices by two brothers who identified themselves as members of al-Qaeda. They killed a dozen journalists, cartoonists and staff and injured eleven more. The magazine, which Steff remembered fondly from his Paris days, had been publishing irreverent cartoons of the Prophet Muhammad, along with, it should be said, articles mocking Catholicism and Judaism and indeed any other group they saw as an affront to personal freedom. No figure of authority was sacred to the paper. He'd been surprised to find that their offices were in the 11th *arrondissement*, just down the road from Oberkampf. A couple of days later, accomplices of the brothers attacked a kosher supermarket in Porte de Vincennes, in the same area, and killed four people, all of them Jewish. Millions of Parisians took to the streets in protest, raising the cry *Je suis Charlie*. Steff was with them in spirit. If there was one thing to hold on to after all the slaughter, it was the spirit of *laïcité*, the separation of all religions from the secular state that was still so strong among so many French people.

The day after he arrived he went on his own pilgrimage to rue Nicolas Appert, where Charlie's work went on. The first edition after the attack sold millions, compared with the thousands they'd sold before. It was an ordinary little street, even a little drab. The same went for the supermarket at the Porte de Vincennes – people going about their daily business, carrying out bags of groceries for the dinners they'd planned that night. Steff couldn't help thinking too, of the round-ups of the Jews in 1942. All of these things, all these atrocious events, happened in his neighbourhood, which, when he first came there, looked like any other. What, he reflected, was done in the name of religion. No doubt it could have its uses – good works, succour to the suffering, help of the helpless as the old hymn had it. But it was what some followers did for their power and glory was where the problem lay. Would the world indeed be better off without it, as John Lennon imagined? Steff thought so. He remembered his Welsh grandmother telling him stories of the fire and brimstone days in chapel when she was a girl. The preacher in his interminable sermons would seem to be transported to a fever pitch and would denounce sinners, usually young women, by name, along the lines of, 'That So-and-So has been up the mountain again – with boys. She will in all certainty feel the flames of Hell.'

It would put the fear of God into the congregation, which Steff supposed was the point. It didn't stop the young from pursuing their natural instincts as they had always done.

He returned home in sombre mood, but consoled himself with a good bottle of wine and the thought that the following night he would at long last meet his cousin.

19

Sebastien had suggested one of his favourite restaurants, Le Vieux Belleville, for their meeting. He advised that they meet early, at six, as there would be music later on and it would give them time to talk. It was near enough for Steff to walk, although it was all uphill to the top of the Parc de Belleville. The new, fitter Steff thought he'd be up to it, and, with a couple of breathers, he got there on relatively good form, although as he approached it he was sweating with nerves.

He recognised his cousin straightaway, sitting at a *table à deux* by the window, sipping a small glass of port. He got up, and Steff went to shake his hand, but he was grasped by the shoulders and kissed three times on the cheeks.

Conversation was perhaps naturally stilted at first – they seemed to have to go through the customary preliminaries, enquiring after each other's health and that of their families and so in. It was only after their artichoke soup had arrived and they'd each had a couple of glasses of wine that they started opening up. Steff took to his cousin from the get-go. He was affable and easy in his skin, easy to talk to.

'So when did you know about us, your aunt's family?' said Steff.

'Well, I only met my mother a few years ago. I think I mentioned to you that I was adopted by a family in Normandy at an early age. Dairy farmers. They didn't tell me that they weren't my natural parents until I was sixteen. They sat me down and told me that I was special, that I was chosen and so on. I have to say it came as a bit of a blow, as you can imagine. But,' and here he gave a familiar Gallic shrug with his palms raised upwards, 'I got over it. I had a happy childhood and loved them very much, and my older sister who was also adopted. I guess they couldn't have children, although that was never stated.'

'So how and when did you find your mother, and us?' said Steff, remembering Esther's request.

'I didn't do anything about it for years, didn't feel the need. And somehow I didn't want to upset things, you know, with my parents, because that's how I thought of them. It was only after my mother died that I began to wonder – you know how you do as you get older – and it started to niggle at me.

'Things had become easier by then. We had the right to our birth certificates, and then there was the internet and so on.'

Their steaks arrived – they had both ordered rare – and there was a slight pause in the narrative, but Sebastien seemed eager to take it up again.

'After quite a bit of detective work I tracked her down to a nursing home in Rouen, you know, where Joan of Arc was burnt at the stake. Funny to think she was living just a few kilometres from where I was brought up. For a long time I pondered about how to approach her. It was bound to come as a shock. In the end I wrote her a letter, just giving my birth date and birth mother's name and saying we might be related. I didn't hear back from her for weeks until I was on the point of giving up hope. If she didn't want anything to do with me, there was nothing I could do. But then a package dropped through the letter box. It had a Rouen postage mark on it. I ripped it open. Inside was a cassette wrapped in a bit of paper. It said. "Dear Sebastien, I've been trying to think how to write all this down, but I couldn't. So I've decided to tell you on this cassette. Céleste Dujardin."

'The words on the tape are etched on my mind. It was a nice voice, softly spoken. She sounded kind. It began, "I remember the day I took you home from the hospital on the bus. The sun was shining on your beautiful white face and I knew that I'd have to give you up." '

Sebastien paused, swallowing hard, as if he was fighting to keep control of himself. It was fortunate that at that point the waiter came to clear their plates and bring the cheese. Once again, he took up his story without any prompting. His mother told him that she was estranged from her family, the father was a bad man, she was a teacher so she couldn't keep the child. It ended with her apologising for causing any anguish and wishing him well.

'It seemed like a sign-off, as if she felt she'd given me all necessary explanation. But I had so many more questions, and, yes, I wanted to meet her. I wrote thanking her, and asked if I could visit her. There was no reply. In a way I felt sorry for her, me coming out of the blue like that, and I didn't want to hound her but there were things I felt I had the right to know. Of course I had a lot of discussions with my wife and she encouraged me. By this time I'd got the number of the nursing home. I got the train to Rouen early one morning – to leave me plenty of time – and rang it from the station. I explained who I was and asked to speak to my mother, saying I was in the town. The carer told me they had no such resident as Mme Dujardin.

'That was a bit of a blow, I can tell you, and it threw me at first. But I was determined to persist. I explained I'd had a letter from her recently, with the sender's address given as that home, with the name Céleste Dujardin. Fortunately the carer seemed helpful and after a pause when she seemed to consult someone else, came back on the line and said they did have someone called Céleste Renault. I took a punt and said that was a name she used sometimes. There was another pause while she seemed to be weighing up her options and she said she would go and see. When she came back she said Mme Renault was not well enough to come to the phone. I left a message that I didn't want to be a nuisance but had a couple of questions and if she didn't want to meet me I'd phone again in a few days. I guessed my first letter must have got through to her somehow.

'Anyway, a couple of days later I got a note from her. She apologised for messing me around, said she could understand that I had a right to know certain things about my birth, but she wasn't in the best of health and she would find it difficult to meet me. However, she said I could come for an hour in the late morning before her lunch and nap. She named a date about a week later. And she congratulated me for tracking her down.'

A man with a huge white handlebar moustache who'd been standing at the bar had gone to the other end of the room to set up his old wooden barrel organ. He handed out song sheets to the diners so they could sing along. The organ worked by feeding cardboard with little slits cut into it, rather like a pianola.

Trois petites notes de musique
ont plié boutique au creux du souvenir

'His name is Riton la Manivelle,' said Sebastien in a low voice, leaning over the table. 'The *manivelle* is the handle on the organ, but it also means someone who's eccentric.'

A crank, thought Steff. He was grateful for the explanation – he wouldn't have got it.

'He's a regular here and quite a character. He plays mainly popular songs – I mean old songs popular with the working class. This one is by Yves Montand, quite a sad song – how three little notes of music you heard in the past can come back and rekindle painful memories.'

Mais un jour sans crier gare,
elles vous reviennent en mémoire.

As the clientele got into the swing of things the singing got louder and conversation became nigh on impossible. They waited for the music to stop.

'It's going to be difficult to talk here. When did you say you were going back to London?'

'The day after tomorrow.'

The singing started up again, with even more gusto: *Sous les Ponts de Paris*. Sebastien nodded at the door, and they got their coats and went outside.

'I'd better be getting back now,' he said. 'I promised my wife I wouldn't be late. Paris can feel quite a dangerous place these days, since the Charlie Hebdo attacks.'

Steff nodded his sympathy

'Could we meet up again tomorrow?' he asked. 'There's still a lot more I'd like to know.'

'Well, I can certainly relate to that. Why don't you come over to our place for an *apéro* so you can meet Afifa, my wife. But I think it's best if we came here again so we can talk frankly. I don't think there's music here tomorrow night.'

'Thank you. I'd like that. But here's another thought. Have you ever seen your mother's flat?'

'No, I never had the chance.'

'Would you like to?'

'Very much.'

'Well, why don't you come round tomorrow afternoon? Then we can go to your place briefly, and then come and eat.'

'That would be great.'

When Steff had got home and heard bangs and then sirens he switched on the news channel to see what was going on. He watched in horror at the unfolding events. There'd been two suicide attacks at the Stade de France, followed by shootings at various cafés fairly nearby. And now there was a siege at the Bataclan concert hall which was just opposite the bottom of Oberkampf. His phone rang. He jumped. It was Esther.

'Where are you?' she demanded without preamble.

'Safe in the flat,' he said.

'Oh, thank the Lord,' she said. 'Are you watching what's going on?'

'Mmm-hmm,' he said, unable to take his eyes off the screen, where police, fire engines and ambulances were blaring outside the Bataclan and the breaking news banners along the bottom were reporting that the death toll was mounting. 'Just got in from meeting Sebastien.'

'Is he OK?'

'Don't know. I was just about to ring him. He was going to take the metro back so he should be alright.'

'It's just too much to take in.'

'I know. It becomes so real when it's on your doorstep and you're watching the live pictures.'

'Well, stay safe.'

'I'm not going anywhere. But don't worry, nothing much can happen to me up here.'

'Well drop me some texts now and again.'

'Will do. Love you.'

'Love you more.' At this, she managed a little sigh

of a laugh, so uncharacteristically schmaltzy it was of them.

Steff rang his cousin's mobile but it went to voicemail. He left the appropriate message, and went on watching until the small hours when the siege at the Bataclan was over. By then ninety fans of the Eagles of Death Metal had been killed in the concert hall, almost a hundred and forty in the city as a whole, hundreds more injured, several of them critically. He lay down on the bed but couldn't sleep. He and Esther talked and texted regularly.

'What is the world coming to?' she kept saying. What could you say about such slaughter?

Sebastien called early next morning. He was safe at home, but his wife Afifa, French-Algerian herself, was distraught.

'But let's stick to our plan. I'll come to the flat about four. I'll have to let you know about coming to our place. I'd love to invite you, but Afifa may not be up to it.'

'Yes, of course, don't worry about it. Are you sure it's OK to leave her?'

'Oh, yeah. We've discussed it. Life goes on. You can't just imprison yourself in your house. I'm going on the principle that lightning doesn't strike in the same place twice.'

'Let's hope so. See you later.'

He rang Esther again, assured her he was OK, and this time he filled her in on his conversation with Sebastien. Both were glad to get back to some semblance of normality. Later that morning he ventured out to the local supermarket to buy port and pretzels and nuts to offer as an aperitif in case they couldn't go to Sebastien's, and a bottle of cognac for good measure. The streets, shops and cafés were noticeably quiet although most places were open and there were people going about their business, looking somewhat stunned. But here they were, out and about. He remembered the public response on the internet to the London bus bombing all those years back: all kinds of people including young children holding up signs saying 'We're not afraid.' Everywhere he overheard murmured talk of the previous night's events, the same kind of incredulous, inexpressible sentiments he'd had with his wife and cousin.

Back in the flat he switched on the news and followed the search for the assailants. Seven of them had either blown themselves up or been killed by the police and anti-terrorists squads. Despite his cousin's words, he was worried about him. He'd worked out that the direct route from his home on the boulevard de la Bastille to Oberkampf was past the Bataclan. But Sebastien was fairly prompt, himself bearing a bottle of Laphroig. They'd both had the same idea.

They began by acknowledging how difficult it was to find something meaningful to say at such times, other than how awful it was, the horror and the sorrow.

'It's always religion, isn't it?' said Sebastien. 'What's done in its name, whichever one it is. Oh, I'm sorry – are you religious?'

'No, I'm a Humanist. I've been thinking along similar lines.'

'Ah. I was brought up a good Catholic, but turned my back on it.'

Steff recounted that years before, when the Middle East was a calmer place, he'd toured monasteries in Egypt, Lebanon and Syria. He'd been struck by their philosophies of sanctuary and hospitality to anyone who needed it. Unless it was a form of proselytism. But surely that was too cynical?

'Yes, and now it seems there's more hate than love,' said Sebastien. 'When did that begin? All this social media seems to be a great spreader of it.'

'Ah, so you're another future denier?'

'A what?'

'A future denier. I saw this documentary about executives of these tech companies. When the interviewer asked one about all the downsides, he accused him of denying the future.'

'Well, let us deny it then. We haven't got all that much of it left, so time becomes more precious. Puts things into perspective. Perhaps it's nature's way of ensuring that we're ready to go when our time comes, that we're wearying of the world and fearing its new ways.'

'At times like this it can feel as if the end of the world is nigh,' said Steff. 'But history is littered with such times. Perhaps it's part of the human condition. Although I can't help feeling that climate change may be leading to the end of it all.'

'And it doesn't matter what religion it is,' said Sebastien, continuing his train of thought. 'Think of your Christians.'

'How'd you mean?'

'In Northern Ireland. Christian against Christian.'

'Oh yes, that hadn't even occurred to me. But there was a lot more to it than that.'

'There always is. Look at what Israel does to its neighbours. The abused will abuse, as they say.'

'That's not a very enlightened view about individuals who've been abused,' said Steff. They exchanged meaningful looks.

'No, you're right. But I've never really understood why the Israelis, or at least most of them, think they can just grab land from over their borders. By some God-given right, I suppose, or a sense of reclaiming their ancient land.'

'And by that token, if we went by the status quo of a couple of thousand years ago, Britain would still be ruled by the Romans. At least in France you have *laïcité*.'

'And look where it gets us.'

Steff nodded sadly.

'I've been wondering – does the Quran tell Muslims to kill non-believers, do you know?'

'I believe it does, in a self-defence kind of way,' said Sebastien. 'But look at the Bible. In Ezekiel it says you should kill your neighbour if he works on the Sabbath. Here endeth the First Lesson.'

'Thank God for us heathens,' said Steff. 'Let's have a drink.'

With a smile at each other they clinked their glasses. Neither for the moment seemed to have much more to say on the subject. Steff often marvelled that all his ancestors, going right back into the void, had survived the wars and plagues and famines and so on, and that he could be here on earth at all.

'Anyway, what do you think of the place?' he said, waving his arm around the room.

'It's strange to be here, thinking that my mother lived here all that time, and hung on to it for years.'

Steff wondered when his cousin had found out about the flat, what he thought of the fact that it had been left to them, and indeed what, if anything, he knew about his father. But all that was probably for later. He gave his cousin a little tour. It was not so unrecognisable from when they'd first arrived, and yet it had a totally different feel. Sebastien admired the way they'd done it up. Steff gave Esther the credit. In the kitchen he showed him the old wooden cabinet he'd bought at the antique shop down the road: a 1940s style called Mado.

'There was one like that in my...our grandparents' kitchen in Conflans. Were you ever there?'

Sebastien was stroking the Mado admiringly, almost as if it was familiar.

'I did go out there a couple of years ago, after I found out the address. It looked as if there was a family living there – toys in the garden and so on – and work being done – new garage and a porch being built. I'd meant to knock on the door and ask if I could have a look around, but somehow I couldn't bring myself to.'

He proffered his glass for a top up, and Steff gladly obliged.

'What was it like?'

'Old fashioned. Lots of heavy wooden furniture, like this cabinet here. Somehow I took a shine to the style.'

He wasn't sure how much to go into about their

grandparents, but told himself it was a time for full and frank disclosure.

'They were an odd couple. Shut up in themselves, if you know what I mean. As if they were just going through the motions.'

'I suppose it must have been quite a sad place after… well, after our mothers left.'

'My mother told me once that it wasn't a happy home. But she didn't seem to want to talk about it much.'

'I got that impression from my mother, too. Vaguely. She didn't talk much either.'

'So you did go and see her?'

'Yes. I went to see her as she suggested. It wasn't an easy meeting.' He paused. 'Tell you what, shall we adjourn to the restaurant. We can talk there. Afifa sends her apologies. She was so looking forward to meeting you, but, well, with what's happened she's not ready to see anyone just yet. Next time, she says.'

'Totally understandable. Give her my regards. And, yes, we have a lot to catch up on.'

20

The Vieux Belleville was quiet, but by no means empty. Chatter was subdued. They sat at the same table by the window, and already it felt like their special one. Riton's organ was stacked against the back wall, and when the waiter came, Sebastien asked him if he was going to perform.

'Yes, around nine. He wasn't due to, but he rang up this afternoon and said he wanted to come in. *Il faut continuer vaille qui vaille.*' The show must go on.

'We'd better get down to business then,' said Sebastien after their orders had been taken. 'I'll tell you anything you want to know. But first, I'd like to hear more about your quest to find my mother.'

Steff had already told him about the photo in the attic, how it aroused his curiosity, especially after his mother was so evasive about the whole subject of her sister. He described his visits to their grandparents in Conflans and how they too would clam up when Céleste was mentioned, how he went to the lycée and then the flat.

'So that's where she was teaching,' put in Sebastien. 'I always wondered.'

'It was only in later years after the death of the grandparents that Maman opened up a little, but was still guarded. That's when she said it was not a happy home. And that was really about it, until we got a letter about the flat. Did you know about that, by the way?'

'Only when I saw the will. By then I did know that there was a sister and a nephew. I respected Maman's decision. I was left the house she had in Rouen. We sold it, and bought a bigger flat overlooking the canal at Bastille. It's really great. We love it there. It's a pity you couldn't have seen it.'

'Next time, maybe?'

'Next time, of course.'

'Anyway, you were going to tell me about meeting up with your mother.'

'Oh yes. Well, that first time I went to the retirement home, it was very strange for both of us, naturally. She was very quiet, and didn't tell me much more than she'd said in that tape. Again, she apologised for giving me away, as she put it, but I assured her I understood she didn't have much choice. Mainly we just kept staring at each other, sort of surreptitiously.

'The home and her room were comfortable enough. It had a nice view down to a little stream. What I noticed, though, was that there seemed to be no personal effects in it – no photos or knick-knacks or little pieces of furniture she might have brought from her own home.'

'What was she like herself?'

'Not as I'd pictured her,' said Sebastien. 'It's odd how you form a mental image of someone you've never met without even realising it. I suppose I saw her as an old-fashioned elderly mother from picture books – you know – a little plump with curly white hair and a flowery dress. She would have been in her early eighties by then. But she had straight cropped grey hair – a nice grey, silvery – and had a good figure, very elegant.'

This description, thought Steff, could equally well have applied to his own mother.

'But there was a sadness in her eyes, her mouth. She spoke softly, briefly. You could sense suffering.' He took a deep breath and changed gear. 'I told her about my life a bit, that I'd had a happy childhood not far from there, that I became a lecturer in literature at the Sorbonne, married Afifa, and had three children and grandchildren. "Muslim?" she asked about Afifa. I said she was Muslim born but not religious. "I hope you're happy together," she said and for the first time gave a little smile, albeit a weak one. I thought I'd caught her wipe away a tear when I was talking about the Sorbonne. I said we were very happy. Good, she said and that sad look clouded her eyes again.

'After an hour or so she stood up and said she needed her afternoon nap. "It was very nice to meet you," she said, and held out her hand. Very formal. I shook it, and didn't want to push my luck, but there was still a lot missing from the story. I appreciated that it wasn't easy for her, but I wanted to get to know her after a lifetime apart. I wanted to hear about her estrangement from the family, and about my father.'

'Ah yes. I've been wondering what you know about him, but didn't quite see how best to ask.'

'We'll get to it,' said Sebastien with a smile. 'I shook her hand, and said I hoped I could call in again sometime to see how she was, and asked her if there was anything she needed. I'm afraid I told a little white lie and said I had some business in the town now and again. She looked at me as if it were a surprising request. Perhaps in her own mind she'd thought she'd told me all I needed to know. She said alright then, she supposed that would be OK if it were brief – she tired easily these days.

'So a couple of weeks later I went to the home, not quite knowing what to expect. But I was shown straightaway to a little terrace at the back where she was sitting in the sun. She stood up, and for a moment I thought we were going to kiss, but I had to wait for her to make the first move. Instead, she held out her hand, we shook, and she suggested we go up to her room for some privacy. This I took as an encouraging sign. But when we got there neither of us seemed to know where to pick up. She asked after my family. Then she said she'd had time to think things over, and that she understood that I may have some questions, and although it was not easy for her she would do her best to answer them.

'I'd been thinking about how to broach the subject of the family, so I started by asking why she left Conflans. She looked out of the window and that misty look came into her eyes. "Well," she said. "I got a teaching job in Paris and a little *deux pièces* nearby. I rented it at first but over time saved up enough to put a deposit down on it." She paused and looked me straight in the eye. She seemed to make up her mind about something. She said it was like being set free, a huge sense of relief. Things were hard at home, especially with her father. She didn't used the word abuse – I suppose you didn't hear that so much back then – but said he did things "I didn't like." She missed her younger sister, and didn't know if she was suffering too. She thought not. She herself was the elder and so he focussed on her. They never discussed it. "We were afraid of what the other one knew," she said. I'm pretty sure that was when I found out about your mother, although she didn't mention her name, maybe out of some sense of protection. I expressed my sympathy, asked her if she wanted to talk about it a bit more, but she said no. She did begin to look wearied. I thought it better not to bring up the question of my father then – on the birth certificate it just said unknown.

'After that we fell into a pattern of visits every other Sunday afternoon. On the third or fourth, we kissed. It was a special thing. My adoptive parents had both died by then. I still hesitated to bring up the question of fatherhood. But after five or six visits we were much easier with each other and it came out more or less naturally. She'd told me that when she found out she was pregnant she was horrified. She had no idea what to do. She seems to have ruled out abortion from the get-go – due to her Catholic upbringing, I suppose, although that didn't stop her having me out of wedlock. But I'm not judging her,' Sebastien was quick to add. 'Far from it.

'She made up her mind to have me adopted, but had no idea how to go about it. She wanted to keep her job. There was no way she was going to ask her parents for help. In the end she went to stay with the family of a fellow-teacher. This was at the start of the long summer break, and before the *rentrée* she told the school she'd been injured and needed a few weeks off work. It was the war, you know, and all kinds of things happened which weren't questioned as they would be today. With the Rouen family's help she arranged the adoption, then went back to the flat and the school. I guess that's how I ended up in the area.

'Anyway at that point, I felt I could ask about the father. I was careful to use the word "the" instead of "my." She sighed and looked directly at me. "Yes, I can see you have a right to know, so I'll tell you. I haven't told this to another living soul." And then the story of my father came tumbling out.'

He paused and took a mouthful of wine.

'I'm sorry this is turning out to be such a long ramble,' said Sebastien. 'Sure you're OK with it?'

'Yes, absolutely,' said Steff. 'This is precisely what I was hoping to know.'

'My father's name was Lucien LaGarde.'

Ah, thought Steff. So it was indeed him.

'My mother took up with him just before the outbreak of war. She soon suspected he was married, although he never told her so. She'd see him mainly at the weekends, always at her flat; she never once visited his home. Occasionally he'd spend the night. But she turned a blind eye – it was love. He was a charmer and she forgave him everything, at least to begin with.

'Gradually she learnt that he was involved with this

antisemitic lot, *Action Française*. She didn't like it, but lumped it, for a while. In fact he was quite guarded about his activities, and she didn't want to know.'

'At this point I should tell you I found out something about him,' said Steff. 'I found a box in the flat with his membership card of the *Action Française*. But I couldn't know for sure he was your father.'

'Good God. Really?'

'Yes. But you go on. I'll fill you in in a minute.'

'OK, well, as the war went on, it became more and more evident that something was happening to Jewish people. They couldn't be seen in bars etc, men started disappearing from the school, for example. Then women and children started disappearing too. At last, she said, the blinkers fell from her eyes and she wanted nothing more to do with him. She told him so. He became nasty, said he knew where she lived, and it wasn't the last she'd see of him. It was about this time that my mother found out about me, and left for Rouen. She had an arrangement with the concierge that if LaGarde came around she'd tell him that Céleste had moved and was not coming back. She put a false name on the letter box.'

An image flashed into Steff's mind of the concierge's lodge at the flat when he went there as a student. It was as clear as daylight. Funny how some memories remain so sharp and others fade away into the haze like will o' the wisps. He was sure she'd denied all knowledge of the aunt while professing her eagerness to help. Could it be that she was protecting Céleste, still mindful of the pact they had entered?'

'Shortly before my mother left,' Sebastien was continuing, 'she saw a young woman jump out of a fourth floor window clutching the hand of her screaming child. It was when they were coming for the Jewish women and children. My mother never told LaGarde about me and never saw him or heard from him again.'

'Whew. Quite a lot to take in,' said Steff. He raised his arm to summon the waiter. 'Let's have some cognac.'

'Good idea. I could certainly do with some.'

'How did you react to all of this – if there are any words?'

'Well, obviously it all came as a shock at first, but then I remember feeling a kind of relief that the truth had been told. Over the couple of years or so I reconnected with her, we'd come to a kind of understanding. After she told me about my father, I was worried that I was the cause of her shame, in case I'd turned out like him and she'd spawned a monster. But she assured me that it was her shame of hooking up with someone like LaGarde in the first place. I think, reading between the lines, that she hadn't always intended to cut herself off from her family entirely, but after she woke up to what was happening with the Jewish people and his role in it, she felt she just couldn't look them in the face again.'

'Well, it must have meant a great deal to her to meet you finally and see how you've turned out. Remind me how you found out about me?'

'I think I told you there was this childhood friend in Conflans who she was in touch with, and was also in touch with my mother. My mother had sworn her to secrecy about her whereabouts, but through her knew that her sister was in England and had a son, a little younger than me. The go-between was dead by then so I didn't have a clue where you were and it took me a while to get round to trying to track you down.'

'I'm so glad you did. For a while after I retired more or less I was feeling sort of lost, empty. And I began to see that I needed a sense of purpose, as indeed we all do. You gave me that purpose, for which I thank you. The quest for the truth, however painful it may be. Sometimes you find things when you stop looking for them.'

'I'm glad too,' said Sebastien, and they clinked glasses. 'I wish we could have met that mutual friend.'

'Yes, that would have been interesting. When I first used to go to our grandparents' house I got friendly with the couple next door and they knew vaguely of a woman who'd known them both as girls but I don't think they could remember her name so nothing came of it.'

'And the grandparents couldn't help?'

'No. Grandmother in particular just clammed up whenever your mother's name was mentioned.'

'Mmm. Not sure whether I blame them or not. Just a sad, sad, story.'

'One other question if I may. Your mother used the name Mme Renault, probably as some kind of sanctuary. Was she ever married?'

'You know, I never really established that. I assume not. The name on her will was Céleste Dujardin. Now, you were going to tell me about what you found in the flat.'

Steff described the shoebox and its contents, including the photo of the baby which must have been taken when he was just a few days old.

'I forgot to bring them with me. I will – next time.'

'Please do – next time.'

Steff summarised the research he'd done at various libraries and memorials, such as Drancy and the Martyrs de la Déportation behind Notre Dame. He'd found out that LaGarde was in league with Louis Darquier, the chief architect and organiser of the deportation. He'd died years ago.

'Fuck,' said Sebastien. 'Did you find out what happened to him?'

'No, couldn't find any mention of him after the war.'

'Well, after D-Day the Germans retreated towards Paris and destroyed whole villages and the inhabitants, so when it was all over, the people took their revenge. Women who'd consorted with the Nazis had their heads shaven and were vilified. Some of the collaborators were brought to justice, but others were shot or hung by mobs.'

'Maybe that's what happened to LaGarde,' said Steff.

'Let's hope so,' said Sebastien, with something between a grimace and a smile. 'No, I take that back. It's descending to his level.' He thought for a moment. 'How swiftly a populace can change, like a flock of birds suddenly swarming in a different direction.'

'More cognac?' said Steff. 'Sorry if that's just rubbing salt into the wound.'

'No, no. More light on the darkness. Better than not.'

'And what do you feel about your father now?'

'Guilty, because I came from him. Proud, because I'm not like him. I've had some low moments, but ultimately there comes a sense of relief in knowing. You kind of make your peace with it.'

Steff's mind turned to his own recent troubles, since his retirement and lack of purpose. He thought of that imaginary gun that he'd used to obliterate bad memories. The most disturbing thing was that often his targets were people he was fond of. Things got a lot better when he'd talked about it with Esther. He slowly came to the realisation that it wasn't people he wanted to obliterate, or himself, but just circumstances: things he had done or left undone, or said or left unsaid. Life's little mistakes. He came to accept that they didn't matter. He'd never had much time for regret. Sebastien's words comforted him, but he couldn't quite bring himself to share his thoughts, as he knew he should. For some reason, they now turned to his grandparents.

'I guess there's no way of knowing what went on in that house in Conflans when our parents were young. But I suppose now I do forgive them for their attitude to your mother, or at least understand it. We all have secrets.'

'That's true. Maybe we're entitled to them. Sometimes we hide them from ourselves.'

'Hmm, but they can eat you up.' Steff was talking to himself as much as to his cousin. He changed tack.

'And are you sure you didn't resent your mother leaving me the Oberkampf flat? It came as a big surprise to us, I can tell you.'

'Oh, on the contrary. I was glad that she was reaching out to the family at last, in some kind of way.'

'That's very…magnanimous of you. We really appreciated it. We've had many happy times there. And, yes, I suppose, as you say, it's some sort of link.'

'That Drancy place sounds something people should see. I've heard about it in a hearsay kind of way – we weren't taught about all this at school – but never thought of going there, to be honest. Now I think I must.'

'Have you been to the memorial near Notre Dame?'

'Nope.'

'That's worth seeing too. It took a long time for all these places to be thought of, and the role of the French authorities to be acknowledged.'

Steff recalled the words of one woman in Auschwitz inscribed there: *Si le monde savait* – if only the world knew.

'Yes, we must know and remember these things. You're a writer – why don't you write something about it.'

'Hmm. Maybe I will. And you can edit it.'

'Hmm. Maybe I will.' They chinked glasses again.

'Now, I've been talking a lot. You've been all over the world. I've explored it mainly in books. What are your favourite places?'

It was a question Steff got asked a lot and one he dreaded. People were disappointed if you went for the obvious, or gave a pat answer like it depends. But if you said too much it sounded like swagger, or a prepared statement.

'Well, let me see. The European cities I like best are

Lisbon, Stockholm and Venice. The most breathtaking sights are the Grand Canyon, the Great Wall of China and Rio Harbour. Three of the most stunning natural beauty places would be the Sahara Desert, the steppes of Mongolia, and the Norwegian fjords – places that can't easily be conveyed in words or pictures.'

'And that's your job.'

'Yes,' said Steff, and the cousins smiled at each other.

'There really are a lot of wonderful things to see on this earth, aren't there? You're lucky to have seen them.'

'Yes, I am,' he said, and thought, 'and I have been, sometimes without realising it.' It was no use saying that travelling for a living also had its drawbacks: hours in airports, nights in soulless hotel rooms, lonely Sunday afternoons.

'And which do you prefer – London or Paris?'

Steff had a ready-made answer for that one.

'I always say London for its character, Paris for its beauty.' And now he remembered that it was what his mother said to him when he first went to the capitals all those years ago.

'Good answer.'

'Do you know it well? London?'

'Haven't been for ages.'

'You and Afifa must come over to stay.'

'Thank you. We'd like that.'

As they exchanged their *aux revoirs* outside, Sebastien said, 'Perhaps you could take me to Drancy one day, as a sort of atonement for the sins of my father.'

'I will.'

From inside came the strains of the song his mother sang to him that faraway day in Conflans: Jean Gabin's *Quand on S'promène au Bord de l'Eau*. Workers escape the drudgery and the "prison" of Paris to walk along the river on Sunday are revitalised by nature's beauty.

Du lundi jusqu'au samedi
Pour gagner des radis
Quand on fait sans entrain
Son boulot quotidien
Subi le propriétaire
Le percepteur, la boulangère
Et trimbalé sa vie de chien
Le dimanche vivement
Qu'on file à Nogent
Alors brusquement
Tout paraît charmant

Quand on s'promène au bord de l'eau
Comme tout est beau
Quel renouveau
Paris au loin nous semble une prison
On a le coeur plein de chansons
L'odeur des fleurs
Nous met tout à l'envers
Et le bonheur
Nous saoule pour pas cher
Chagrins et peines
De la semaine
Tout est noyé dans le bleu dans le vert.

From Monday to Saturday
To earn peanuts
We're down in the dumps
Doing our daily jobs
Hassled by the landlord
The taxman, the baker
And leading a dog's life
We can't wait for Sunday
When we can go to Nogent
Then all of a sudden
Everything looks lovely

When we walk along the water
What a delight it all is
How we're revitalised
Faraway Paris seems like a prison
Our hearts are full of song
The scent of flowers
Turns us topsy-turvy
And happiness
Gets us drunk on the cheap
Troubles and sorrows
Of the week
Are all drowned in blue and green.

21

'What now?' Esther had asked over supper upon Steff's return. He'd filled her in on the meetings with his cousin, and the story of his aunt. She'd listened eagerly, and said, 'It's fascinating how the pieces came together after all these years.'

'What do you mean – what now?'

'Well, now that your quest is over. Do you feel some kind of...,' she'd hesitated a second or two, '... anticlimax?'

Steff had interpreted this to mean she was worried he might slide back into his dark place, now that he'd found what he'd been looking for.

'No, I don't, as it happens. It's good to know the truth, or as much of the truth as can be known. It's filled a void. And I've got Sebastien. It means I'm no longer alone.'

'And what am I, chopped liver?'

'Oh, you know what I mean. I realise now that it did feel lonely being in the dark about Céleste.'

'I'm kidding, hon.' She'd put her hand over his. 'I understand completely.'

'Sebastien and Afifa would love us to go over to stay with them sometime.'

'And I'd love that too.'

And here they are, the four of them sitting on the balcony overlooking the Canal Saint Martin below the Bastille in the early evening sun, sipping kirs.

'I still don't understand why she hid that box under the bath,' says Esther. They've been talking about Céleste and her sad, lonely life.

Steff looks at Sebastien, who says, 'Maybe it was a sort of *mea culpa* – acknowledging her guilt for hooking up with that bastard, for giving me away, for turning her back on her family. It was her atonement.'

The others nod slowly in agreement.

'How tragic it is in life when you can't be who you are,' says Afifa. It's Esther and Steff's second night staying with them. They both took to her immediately. She's gentle and smiling and couldn't have made them feel more welcome. She's tiny, her hair still dark, her lips lush scarlet, and she's wearing a simple black dress.

It's about a year after the Bataclan attacks, and a pall still hangs over the city. It's a sadder place than it used to be. But in the setting sun, it's bathed in a golden glow.

'How beautiful,' says Esther, looking over the sparkling water to the spires of Notre Dame. 'The City of Light.'

Steff and Sebastien exchange surreptitious glances. They're thinking that it has its dark places too, its shadows. Afifa knows what they're thinking.

'It's had its share of suffering and sorrow,' she says.

'But it always seems to rise from the ashes.'

The words and music of *Quand On S'promène Au Bord de L'eau* enter Steff's head.

They finish their drinks, and go in through the french windows to the dining room and the tagine that she's prepared.

ACKNOWLEDGEMENTS

Many people merit my heartfelt thanks for their help and support in the writing of Parisian Shadows: firstly my wife Julia, especially for sharing the story of finding her birth mother. I also had valuable suggestions and encouragement from my brother Milwyn, Lida Radkowsky, Victoria Neumark-Jones, Merryn Jones and Tom Keller. I'm indebted as always to my trusty editor, Annabel Hughes and thank you Jerry Timmins for your help.